SUPER PAC

NINE-DAY SHADOW

Book 2 of the Parker Moore Series

SUPER PAC

NINE-DAY SHADOW

A Citizens United Horror Story

STEWERT JAMES

MITCHELL STREET PRESS
PETOSKEY, MICHIGAN
WASHINGTON D.C.

Mitchell Street Press
Petoskey, Michigan
Washington D.C.

www.stewertjames.com

DISCLAIMER: This is a work of fiction. Names, characters, places, and incidents either are the product of the author's imagination or are used fictitiously. Any resemblance to actual persons, living or dead, businesses, events, or locales is entirely coincidental.

James, Stewert.
Super PAC nine-day shadow: a citizens united horror story/Stewert James. — Petoskey, Mich. : Mitchell Street Press, c2014.

p. ; cm.
(Parker Moore series ; book 2)
ISBN: 978-0-9885011-2-6

1. Political action committees—United States—21st century—Fiction. 2. Campaign funds—United States—Fiction. 3. Elections—United States—21st century—Fiction. 4. United States—Politics and government—2009—Fiction. 5. Politicians—United States—Fiction. 6. Lobbying—United States—Fiction. 7. Foreign agents—United States—Fiction. 8. Citizens United—Fiction. 9. United States. National Security Agency—Fiction. 10. Political fiction. I. Title. II. Series.

PS3610.A4547 S862 2014 2013953826
813/.6—dc23 1401

Printed in the United States of America
Third Printing

COVER & INTERIOR DESIGN BY TO THE POINT SOLUTIONS
www.tothepointsolutions.com

To Mom

SUPER PAC

NINE-DAY SHADOW

1

FRIDAY ~ OCTOBER 21

It was an unusually warm Friday evening in late October. Sam was out of town visiting her new grandson; Parker was enjoying the sounds of the wind howling and a dry martini (instead of his usual Lagavulin single malt) while working on a charcoal drawing in his studio. His fingers were black and the floor was covered in discarded sketches.

"Damn!" he yelled as the unexpected sound of the phone ringing caused him to make a mistake on the tree he was sketching. "What the hell?" He grabbed a paper towel and ran upstairs to answer it.

"Mr. Moore?"

Parker did not recognize the male voice.

"Yes?" Parker said as he wiped his hands on the paper towel. The phone was balanced between his shoulder and his ear.

"May we meet for coffee tomorrow, at Roast and Toast? I have a business proposal to share with you." The voice was matter-of-fact; without emotion.

"Well, sure. Who am I speaking with?" Parker knew he sounded hesitant.

"This is Mark Fairchild. Senator Stimson gave me your name before he died."

Stimson? The Super PAC? Now what? thought Parker. The last time he saw Stimson was four years ago in Washington D.C. Since then, Parker had been shot, watched his ex-wife be assassinated, and Stimson died in a plane crash.

"Mr. Moore? Can we meet tomorrow morning?"

"Sure. Sure. About nine?"

"Very well. I will see you there. I'll know who you are." The mystery man ended the call.

Parker looked at the phone as he placed it on the counter next to the stove. After throwing the paper towel into the trash, he turned and walked to the sliding glass door and onto the side deck. He looked toward Lake Michigan then closed his eyes and breathed deeply into the fall wind coming off the lake. As he opened his eyes, he contemplated calling Sam but didn't. No reason to alarm her.

Whoever it was probably knew everything about Parker. Before he found quiet in Harbor Springs a couple years ago, his life had been public; then after the shooting, well, everybody found him—even those he didn't want to.

Living in Petoskey for the last year, Parker had fallen into a nondescript routine: he worked a few hours each day for a local health care group, volunteered for a couple nonprofits in town, took care of his mother's house an hour away on the Manistee River, and helped with his father-in-law who lived in Petoskey. Parker was just beginning to forget his past.

He looked down and saw their two cats weaving between his legs, looking for their dinner. "Come on, Keeper. You too, Kali. Let's get some grub." Parker walked back into the house.

2

SATURDAY ~ OCTOBER 22

Parker got up the next morning and made his way into the dressing room. He grabbed his cap from Jackson Hole, Wyoming, the one with a string hanging down from the bill; slipped on a pair of blue jeans with holes in the knees; and threw on an old sweatshirt from Deer Park Lodge in the U.P. He wasn't into dressing up for anyone except Sam, and he surely wasn't dressing up for a meeting at Roast and Toast on a Saturday morning. If he did, Bob or Mary might wonder what was going on.

After brushing his teeth and checking the Red Wing hockey score from the night before, he walked out the front door, down the steps lined with potted mums, and out into a sunny morning. The leaves of the trees along the boulevard were a vivid red mixed with orange and yellow. Lake Michigan was quiet compared to last night during the strong westerly wind.

Parker walked down Mitchell Street and waved at Mark as he passed the Center City Gym. He turned the corner at the Chamber of Commerce and bolted in to say hello to Sam's friend Kathi.

"Parker! When's Sam coming back?" Kathi asked.

"Next Saturday. Sunday dinner after she returns?" Parker was always pushing for a Sunday dinner with guests. Sam loved them, but she never knew who Parker had invited. One time six people she'd never met showed up.

"You got it." Kathi hugged Parker good-bye.

The streets were empty compared to summer weekends. The fall colors brought tourists up north, but most were retired. The younger families that vacationed here in July and August were back home, running between their kids' football, soccer, and hockey games.

Parker walked toward Symons General Store and stopped at the steps leading to the porch of the popular landmark. The old wooden bench and Coke machine were in their ever-present places. Chandler Symons was just entering the store with his five-year-old son, Tommy, in tow.

"Hey, Chandler. Dinner tomorrow? Hi, Tommy."

"Sorry, Parker. Mom's got us booked." Chandler was holding the screen door open for Tommy.

"Next time, then?"

"Sure, Parker. See you later." Chandler let the screen door bang behind them.

Parker was whistling with nervous energy as he crossed the street and passed Cutler's. By the time he reached Papa Lou's bar, he was outright angry; girded for battle. His senses were on fire. Actually, he was pissed off. Who the hell was waiting for him? What the hell was waiting for him? It was supposed to be done. Over. In the past.

He came upon the famous coffee house with the many colored coffee cups cemented into the arch of the doorway. He looked inside before he entered. He didn't notice anything out of the ordinary.

"Hey, Parker!" shouted Mary from behind the coffee roaster. She was watching the beans for Chuckie while he went downstairs for coffee bags.

"Hi, Mary. How's Bob?" Parker replied.

"Good. Good. He's busy with City Park today," Mary said as she put her head down and looked at the coffee beans turning in the roaster.

City Park Grill was Petoskey's most famous stop on the Hemingway tour. Ernest would often sit at the bar and write when he visited family at the nearby resort area of Walloon Lake. Bob was co-owner of the Grill, along with the Palette Bistro and Roast and Toast.

Parker looked around as he talked with Mary to see who might be waiting for him. He purposely arrived five minutes late to show he wasn't worried or concerned. He spotted a well-dressed gentleman sitting at the first table next to the stairs staring at him with a smile. Just like the old days, he thought. Parker walked over to the table.

"Mr. Moore, I presume?" the man said as he stood up and put his right hand out to shake.

"Mr. Fairchild. I hope you don't mind my leisure attire. This is my Saturday best." Parker really didn't care what Fairchild thought, he was only being polite.

"Of course not. Please, join me." Mark Fairchild sat down as he pointed to the chair across from his.

"Sure. Let me get my coffee first. Anything for you?" Parker asked.

"No. And your coffee is paid for, along with whatever else you want. Just tell the young lady at the counter."

Parker turned and saw Mary at the counter.

"What can I get you, Parker?" Mary asked; then she quietly whispered through her smile, "What's going on? He's been here an hour waiting for you. You're not getting shot again, are you?" Mary smiled and looked at Parker as she reached behind her and grabbed a black coffee mug. "You're gonna be banned if you get shot again." Mary was practically laughing through her teeth.

"Thanks, Mary." Parker said in a normal voice. Then he quietly replied, "No. I'm not getting shot. I don't know who he is."

Parker walked over to the coffee carafes and filled the mug with his favorite, Tanzanian Peaberry.

"So, what can I do for you, Mr. Fairchild?" Parker asked as he sat in the wooden chair. On the wall behind Mark Fairchild hung drawings made by St. Francis elementary students.

"To alleviate any anxiety you may have, let me dispel the danger. I'm here for information. I work for Senator David Henry of Georgia. He's the chair of the Senate Select Committee on Intelligence in charge of investigating Senator Stimson's death."

Parker just stared at Fairchild. The man was probably six feet and weighed two hundred pounds. His shoulders and chest belied the office jockey stereotype and his complexion and features weren't exactly WASP. When Parker heard Stimson's name, he recalled the conversation he had had with the late senator in the Senate Majority office at the Capitol in Washington D.C. Parker guessed something was underneath Stimson's soliloquy that day in 2008, and knew there was a connection to Stimson's death and the National Security Agency's work with the Super PAC.

"Death? He died in a plane crash, right?" Parker played dumb.

"Yes. A plane that landed in the middle of Brooks Range in a million pieces after blowing up in midair. A fact that never made the front pages." Fairchild brought his coffee cup to his lips as he quietly relayed the information.

"Well, now."

"Mr. Moore—Parker. We know you were the last lobbyist to talk with Stimson prior to his trial and conviction. We also know you were wired. What we don't know is for whom and why, and that's why I'm here." Fairchild sat back in his chair with his hands in his lap as he looked around the room. His voice was soft but direct. He turned his gaze toward Parker and waited for an answer.

"I can't help you, Mr. Fairchild—Mark," Parker said sternly as he stood up, turned around, and began to walk toward the door. If he knew everything, he wouldn't be asking questions. Parker was suspicious of the man's motives, and definitely didn't want to have a conversation around people he knew.

"I'm not leaving Petoskey until you give me some answers, Moore."

Parker stopped and turned around. "You'll find nice lodging at the Perry. Brunch in the Rose Room on Sunday is always the best. Starts at ten. Very quiet." Parker winked and left the coffee house.

He walked swiftly down Lake Street, south through Pennsylvania Park, past Meyer's ACE Hardware, and up Mitchell Street past the library, and back home. He caught his breath as he sat in the Adirondack on the front lawn. "Asshole. What the hell is this about?" he mumbled as he watched the few cars that drove by.

3

"I think he's scared," said Pierre Simon into the phone. He stood at a window overlooking the bay on the fourth floor of his room at the Bay Harbor Hotel. "No. No. I still think I'll get to him. He'll be at the Perry Hotel for brunch tomorrow," Simon paused as he listened. "I know he'll be there. Maybe he just needed a night." He paused again. "Well, okay. I'll let you know."

Pierre Simon didn't look much like Mark Fairchild, but the business he was in Petoskey for wouldn't take long. He stood on the balcony and looked across Little Traverse Bay toward Harbor Springs. His glass with a shot of bourbon on ice clinked as he stirred it around with his left hand.

Parker was watching the Detroit Tigers battle the Texas Rangers in game five of the American League Championship series. Verlander was into his one hundredth pitch … Parker wondered what his life would have been like if his arm hadn't been injured when he played Adray ball in Detroit.

His phone beeped. He picked it up off the side table next to the couch and read the text:

Northern lights are out. Huge!

It was his friend Mike, who lived north of Harbor Springs. Parker quickly went outside to the front yard and immediately saw the aurora dancing overhead. He dashed through the house and out the back, hopped into his car, and drove the short distance to East Park. Sam phoned as he drove down US-31.

"Sam, they're beautiful. I wish you were here."

"Me, too! I'm so jealous. I can't see them here," Sam said as she stepped outside from her daughter's house in Idaho Falls.

"Let me call you back," Parker said as he pulled into the park entrance. Other cars were already pulling in behind him.

He walked up the grassy knoll and toward the edge that looked over the water. He heard the surf below. The Aurora Borealis was magnificent. Lights danced from as far west, east, and north as he could see. Harbor Springs looked as if it was being showered in an alien rain made of crystal fibers.

Parker texted his three kids to let them know what was happening. Then his gaze caught the Bay Harbor Hotel. He had no idea where Fairchild was staying, but he glared at the hotel and wondered about the meeting in the morning. He knew Fairchild understood his message about brunch at the Perry. Parker wasn't sure what to expect—but, it was going to be okay. He just knew it was going to be okay. After watching Mother Nature's light show for about half an hour, he left for home. He called Sam as he drove.

"Sam? Are you having a good time with your grandson? … Good. … I've got a meeting in the morning. … Miss you, too. …"

Simon was sitting on the balcony, enjoying a second glass of bourbon and watching the Northern Lights in amazement. He'd never seen them before. There was nothing like it on his native island of Corsica in the Mediterranean.

4

Unable to sleep, Parker got out of bed at 2:00 a.m. He sat in his studio in the basement on the brown stool at the writing table. A small desk lamp was bent down and illuminated the top of the desk. Parker's head rested on his open left hand while his right kept a pen moving a steady stream of words onto paper.

His life sat before him. The Tootsie Toy steel boats his father played with as a child during World War II, Parker's first Matchbox cars, the last trophy won by the championship softball team his family put together with all of the hardball talent, a handful of rocks from various hikes along Lake Superior, maps, notes, paperweights, and an empty bottle of Lagavulin.

As he stopped writing and looked around at the objects he wondered what was the draw. Obviously he kept favorites, but he also held onto items he could discard. Like the empty bottle … but he could remember every word of every poem he wrote while drinking his two fingers' worth. He worried about drinking so much then … He smiled remembering the bottle lasted over a month.

To the side of the table hung jackets and jerseys. The first warm-up of his high school baseball coaching career. His signed Chris Osgood jersey—Osgood was a favorite underdog player who fought adversity from fans and critics to win three Stanley Cups. Behind that was his daughter's soccer jersey from when she played in Toronto. Her high school team would always make the finals only to be jobbed by a homer referee calling the game for the hometown Canadian team. His son's college hockey jersey—the captain's number that took his team to the National Championship in Rochester, New York in 2009.

Below the jerseys, were baseball gloves. His father's left-handed catcher's mitt used to catch twelve-year-old Parker's fastball. His dad's hands became sore, so the sports shop had to order the rare left-handed receiver's glove. Under that one, the glove Parker used at his last pro-invite tryout. The one when his arm gave out. His coaches used Parker three days a week to pitch with no ice, no rest. At twenty-three, the curveball would still fall off a table and the slider would still slide three feet, but there was no fastball to set the table. No velocity. He was done before he ever really got going.

Pictures, fishing equipment, books, drawings—the things Parker kept to remember, but his greatest difficulty was that he couldn't forget.

The humiliation he experienced four years ago, when he finally ended his abusive marriage and gave everything up. Life, home, career—because he broke under stress. He remembered every detail of the final curtain call, but not the absurdity and horrible times before that, when he stuffed the bad away in a remote part of his brain in order to survive. Now the brief memories came as flashbacks and jaw-tightening mystery. Living in a dissociative vacuum caught up to him and six months of his life is a blank.

To regain his sanity, to find himself, Parker began to write. As things cleared, he realized he'd moved to Harbor Springs and now lived in Petoskey—a rebuilt man. He finally *felt*. There were only short bursts of emotion that haunted the present and blinded thoughts of the future.

He returned to writing, while Gordon Lightfoot sang in the background on Parker's now ancient cassette player. Some of Lightfoot's darkest songs that added bleakness to Parker's mood.

He looked up to pause. There was his raven. If you felt like Poe wrote, you needed a big blackbird staring down at you. Especially a stuffed one that never stopped glaring. What would the hours later in the morning bring? The abuse. The lost opportunities. The guttural resentment of a system that crucified him and keeps trying to kill him.

Except for the one six month period, nothing forgotten. He wished his photographic brain would just die. It made college easy.

He rarely attended class, but just showed up for the exams and passed. It made his career easy, but people were always suspicious because Parker never had to show his work. He just made things happen. Now, he wished the pictures would just disappear. It would be so peaceful.

A meeting at a coffee shop and a dead man's name.

Parker looked at the dead bird. "Well, at least Stimson's at peace. He's not stuffed like you, but at peace just the same. 'Nevermore. Nevermore.'"

Back to writing.

Back to the bird.

"You know Stefanie's at peace. Her brain may still be on the pavement in Lansing, but she's at peace. Well, let's hope Virgil has her with Dante and they're going *down* the steps from purgatory. Do you understand anything I'm saying? I didn't think so."

Maybe it was Parker's turn. Maybe he was destined for the same path. Homer's *Iliad and Odyssey*, through the life of Odysseus, was a perfect metaphor for Parker's life: the Trojan horse, the Sirens and Cyclops, even the landing and hiding as someone else. Time travels thousands of years, but the human experience remains the same.

Parker went upstairs in the black of early morning and grabbed the Macallan Fine Oak 10 year old scotch from the cupboard. The whiskey took the place of guns and daggers. It soothed the pain. Just enough to take him to the edge but rarely to the tipping point. He poured himself a glass and carried it back to the study.

The sherry flavors of this Speyside single malt brought pleasantness to the palate. Parker grabbed the empty Lagavulin bottle. "Why you? Why do I love the way you taste even though it's like a ball of peat moss held together with seaweed?" He felt like Hamlet talking to a skull.

The heavy peat and seaweed of the Islay malt would be like pouring gasoline on a fire whereas the Speyside smoothness at least tried to temper the angry soul.

In any case, scotch helped the mood pass; eased the relentless memory.

Three a.m. Both sides of the cassette had played and Gordon

Lightfoot was silent. Parker fingered through his collection of old music and found *Common Thread*, a mix of country stars singing songs by the Eagles. This would continue to add to the depressive mood. Apropos. It was that or George Winston—vocals won out over piano solos.

He picked up his red Formula One Matchbox car and remembered the day his father gave it to him. It came in a tiny box; not a cheap plastic bubble. And it was a Lindsey made in England die-cast model. Nowadays the toys were manufactured in Asia with cheap labor.

He wished Sam was home. She would know when to say something and when not to. Parker didn't have many dark moods anymore; when he did, she just hugged him.

Another sip and Parker looked up toward the window. Shakespeare quotes, Robert Traver trout memories, and Isaiah 41:10: "Fear not; for I am with thee." Everything in the studio was at an eye's reach to keep him going. A castle in a dungeon of life, where everything he owned and cherished stood fast.

Tanya Tucker was singing her version of "Already Gone."

What will happen tomorrow? Later this morning?

How can one phone call and the mention of a name from the past create such stir from the deep recesses of a soul thought healed? It was not for Parker to conclude but only ponder and experience. He'd practiced surrender, giving his beliefs to the rhythms of a vast Universe and Nature to help guide him through this wonder called life. No more histrionic reactions. No more projections into a morass of an abusive world. A surrender to find peace. An acknowledgement of why he kept the past around him in his studio. It grounded him. It made him think and pause. It would act as John's Revelation in the Bible—a cacophony of thought that would eventually lead to quiet.

He emptied the bottle of Macallan. As he wrote with his fountain pen, the letters and words became more difficult to read, but the thoughts were deeper and clearer. He understood why Hemingway and Mozart sank into alcoholic hazes of creation and wondered if that was his destiny. If it was, at least people would remember him.

At around 4:30 a.m., Parker Moore was planning his funeral. The only reason his humiliations of the past had resurfaced was to kill him. To finally put his tortured mind to rest. Secrets he kept that if people knew, they would kill him. The things he had seen and heard. The shackles on his voice only broke on parchment and canvas. No one would believe him.

Haunted minds
Sorrowed souls
Borrowed thoughts
Memories resurface
Harbingers of death
Harbingers of reality
Depression or sanity
What a late night brings
Memorabilia from a millennium
Why does one keep pain?
Depths of despair find comfort
Present realities rekindle the old
Death would bring such sweet peace

Parker wrote loose phrases and thoughts. He attempted to intertwine them into a verse.

He drank the last of the scotch and looked at the rest of the quote from Isaiah:

"... Be not dismayed
For I am thy God.
I will strengthen thee
Yea I will help thee."

Clint Black's version of "Desperado" was playing. Parker put down the pen and sat back in his chair. Soon, he fell asleep.

5

SUNDAY ~ OCTOBER 23

"Kali, what the hell are you doing?" Parker had one eye open. He was lying in bed and looking at the cat as she sniffed his nose. Keeper meowed by his feet. They wanted out. Parker realized he was in bed—after a staggered early-morning walk up the stairs from the scotch-laden studio. "Okay, okay. Let's go."

Parker threw off the covers and looked at the clock. 6:35 a.m. NPR was playing soft New Age music. He stood, stretched, and walked down the hallway and stairs.

A car screeched its tires on Mitchell Street; Parker paid no attention. As he walked into the kitchen, the cats were already waiting at the back door.

"What? Neither of you can open the door?" Parker opened it and in the darkness he saw something slumped over the deck railing. It was too large to be a skunk or a raccoon.

With the movement of the door, the body fell in a heap and knocked down the grill. Parker turned the light on and ran outside into the misty morning.

"Hey? Hey are you awa—?" Parker stopped the second he saw the bullet hole in the forehead of the man. It was Fairchild.

Realizing there was a dead man on his deck, Parker remembered hearing the car screeching out front; he walked into the house, grabbed his cell phone off the counter, and called 911. "Yes. This is Parker Moore at 982 East Mitchell Street. I just found a dead body on my deck. Yes, ma'am. I'll be right here. No, there is no one else around." As he finished the call, Parker heard sirens coming from everywhere.

"Shit," was all he said as he looked down at the corpse.

6

Public safety officers were all over the house and yard looking for any piece of evidence when Tim Johnson, Director of Public Safety, drove up from the back alley. "Moore, why don't you move to Siberia?" Johnson said as he walked onto the deck.

"Sorry, Tim. The Russians won't have me," Parker said without taking his eyes off the body. Cameras flashed while Johnson stood next to Parker and took in the scene.

"Another person from your past? Let's go inside."

Parker turned as Kali and Keeper ran through his legs, into the dining room, and upstairs—their usual hiding place whenever the vacuum came out of the closet or anyone they didn't know entered the house. Parker and Johnson went into the front living room. Johnson sat on the sofa and Parker in the wooden side chair.

"So?" Johnson started.

"The guy, Fairchild, calls me the other day. Um, Friday. And wants to meet me at Roast and Toast; so I go." As Parker tells the story, he quickly reviews his history in his mind before he says each word. He always wonders how much he should say; especially now, with a dead man on his deck. "We talk and he brings up stuff from four years ago that's down the river and out to sea in my head. Said he worked for a senator from Georgia. Henry. David Henry."

"Did he threaten you?"

"No. No. Well, he did say he wasn't leaving town until he got answers, or something like that; but I didn't feel threatened."

Just then an officer walked into the living room. "Director, you might want to see this."

Johnson looked at Parker and stood up. "Just wait here. I'll be right back."

Johnson went through the sliding glass door onto the deck where other officers were looking through the contents of the dead man's pockets. The sun was just poking through the clouds and the fog was starting to lift from Lake Michigan.

7

As the plane sat on the tarmac at Pellston Airport, twenty minutes north of Petoskey, the man sitting in the black Buick in the parking lot sent a text:

Good morning. Job done. Coming home.

A reply came in:

Stay put. Another on the way. Next Saturday here 3:00 p.m.

The charter flight would have to be cancelled.

Todd Ramsey grew fond of Parker Moore two years ago, when he was working alongside John Brooks. Since then, he and Brooks had been sent to Yemen to track cyber intelligence around money, connected to a suspected OPEC-based political action committee in Sana'a, Yemen's capital. This was different than the Super PAC the NSA was a part of. The NSA group didn't take money, and the political influence was through secrecy. When they first started the assignment, Ramsey would not have believed Brooks would be kidnapped—after being set up by an informant—and that he would be back shadowing Moore for a related reason. All Ramsey knew was a code had been broken and cyber chatter from the Middle East revealed three contract killings and money changing hands for political influence in the U.S. Parker Moore's neighbors had checked out clean; so it should be easy to notice someone new in town who was getting near to him. Whoever was after Moore might not make the same mistake twice.

Agent Ramsey knew he didn't have to talk to the charter pilot to cancel the flight; in fact, before he restarted the car, the small jet was leaving the tarmac and heading for the runway.

Ramsey drove out of the airport parking lot and headed south on US-31 toward Petoskey. He had no idea who he was looking for. All he knew is he had one week.

8

Lights and sirens from the first responders' vehicles had awakened the neighborhood. People gathered on all sides of the yard, straining to see and hear all that they could. Unfortunately for them, it was not enough to answer any questions.

"That's a .22 caliber Walther with a suppressor, otherwise known as a silencer. And no, it's not the .32 caliber James Bond style PPK." Johnson was giving Parker a lesson on the gun lying with the rest of the contents from Fairchild's clothing. Before working in Petoskey, Johnson spent time in Iraq and Kuwait as an MP for the Michigan National Guard. "It's mostly used by European and Asian security forces—and only for close quarters. I suspect this guy isn't who you think he is."

Parker, quiet and pensive, suddenly realized his senses had been totally wrong about this morning's meeting being okay. He tried to control his affect to not show emotion. "You think he's here for me?"

Johnson looked up and said factitiously, "Moore, a guy doesn't come to Petoskey with a piece like this to hunt deer. What do you think and what more do you know?" Johnson's smiling face had turned serious.

"I don't know what to tell you. I thought all of this ended in Lansing, at Omar's." Parker felt Johnson's gaze, but he wasn't going to say anymore. Once again, Parker didn't know who he could trust.

"Well," Johnson started as he knelt next to the body and looked through Fairchild's stuff for ID, "there's nothing else here but some gum wrappers and a matchbook from Bay Harbor. I guess we'll start there."

Frank Mehan, the M.E., had finished with his preliminary exam. “I put the time of death at about six,” he said. It was now close to eight thirty. “One shot to the forehead. Bigger than a .22 I’d say, but we’ll need some help to confirm. I don’t handle this kind of thing very often. From the blood on the outside of the deck and on the grass, I’d say the shot came from over there by the street or beyond.”

“Thanks, Frank. I’ll have the State guys assist.” The Petoskey State Police Post already had officers on the scene.

Forensics continued while Parker and Johnson walked inside.

“Parker, tell me you didn’t do this,” Johnson said as they walked through the dining room and back into the front room.

The house was over one hundred years old and Parker often referred to the front area of the house as The Parlor. The hallway entrances were arched and the moldings around the windows and doorframes were original in their preserved Victorian wood and design. Sam and Parker would often walk around the house and wonder what life would have been like in the late 1800s. He wondered if anyone else was ever questioned in The Parlor about a dead body.

“You know better than that. No. I was upstairs, in bed. Wait—I did hear a car screech out front; seemed an unusual time.”

“Where’s Sam?” Johnson sat in the chair by the front door, with his legs crossed and wearing his trench coat.

“She’s in Idaho.” Parker sat in his wooden side chair.

“How’s the new grandson?” Johnson rubbed his eyes with his right hand.

“He’s great. Can we not call her just yet?” Parker was measuring his every move.

“That’s between you and her. By the way, you still drinking that heavy scotch, what’s it called Lagalulu or something?”

“Lagavulin. Yes. Why, do you need some?”

“Later. I’ll come by and we can really talk.” Johnson got up and started toward the front door. He turned. “Don’t go anywhere today. I’ll be back later. These guys will be back and forth all day I’m sure. Oh, and no reporters. Got it?” Johnson was much like his predecessor—untrusting of the press.

"Whatever you say, Tim."

Johnson shut the door while Parker was still answering.

The black Buick drove down Mitchell Street in front of Parker's house as most of the squad cars were leaving. No one noticed.

The boarding house across the street and just west of Sam and Parker's home was a mid-eighteenth century building with a poor attempt at a Victorian paint job. Legend said it was the original hospital in town. The stairs on the front porch were so antiquated they were roped off so people wouldn't fall off.

A woman stood outside on the second-floor balcony, watching while she talked on the phone.

9

Ramsey asked for another room at Stafford's Perry Hotel. The yellow hotel sat at the north edge of downtown Petoskey, and most rooms on the west side had beautiful views of Lake Michigan. Ramsey explained to the desk clerk his flight out of Pellston had been cancelled. The clerk thought nothing of his return and re-registered Mr. Jones into room 310.

Legend has it that 310 is haunted. Numerous guests have encountered apparitions of a woman and a child while staying in that room.

Ramsey wasn't worried about a ghost; but he was concerned about a spook following Parker Moore. He liked the room because of its view, not only of Little Traverse Bay, but also of the main road, the Gaslight District downtown, and the harbor.

"How's the book coming, Mr. Jones?" asked the clerk.

"Good. Good. I figure my flight being cancelled is an excellent reason to stay longer and find more information." Ramsey had a briefcase of research materials and books on the Great Lakes to strengthen his cover.

"Here's your key, sir." The clerk looked up from the computer and handed the key to Ramsey.

Ramsey walked up the enclosed staircase and opened the door to his well-decorated Victorian room, which dated back to 1899. He opened the balcony door, turned, and set his travel bag on the floor. He sat on the edge of the bed then lay on his back, knees at the bottom edge of the bed with his feet still on the floor. He reached above his head to grab a pillow. He placed it under his head and shut his eyes. As he relaxed, he reached under his jacket and dropped his weapon to the floor. It was still missing a bullet.

The sun had finally broken through thin clouds and the fog was totally gone from over the lake. Parker wanted to get away from the hustle and bustle; so he went downstairs and sat at his writing table. He rolled one of his old baseballs from high school back and forth on the table as he thought.

"Why would Stimson give my name out?" he said out loud. "Why would some guy ask about a dead senator from Alaska—and why does anyone care about what I'm doing on Mitchell Street in Petoskey, Michigan, a million miles away from anything political?" He began to roam through the last few days in his head. What did he miss? What was suspicious or out of place? Who was new?

The ball rolled off the table as he remembered a conversation.

Johnson sat at his desk. He was going over information with his officers as quickly as it came in. There was no way he could keep this from the press—but why was there a probable professional hit man in town and why and who professionally killed him?

The body was on its way to the Michigan State Police Forensic Lab in Gaylord, about one hour southeast of Petoskey. The information at Bay Harbor was not helpful. Room paid with cash. No luggage. No car in the parking lot was identified as the victim's.

Fairchild, or whoever he was, was a ghost. Just like Parker was when he dropped into Harbor Springs four years ago. The phone ringing broke his train of thought.

"Johnson," he said into the phone.

"Director Johnson?"

"Yes. Can I help you?"

"This is Special Agent Jack Fletcher from the Washington D.C. FBI office. You called about a Mark Fairchild. Can I ask why?"

"Yes. We had a man who verbally identified himself as Mark Fairchild and said he worked for Senator David Henry from

Georgia. I placed a call to that office in D.C." Johnson was sitting straight up in his chair, waiting for a reply.

"Director, Mark Fairchild was found dead two days ago in his apartment in the Foggy Bottom District of D.C. He was poisoned."

Tim Johnson was silent. He put his head down and ran his left hand through his hair from front to back and tensed.

"Johnson?"

"Poisoned. Wow." Johnson stared into the empty space between himself and the wall. "Any leads or ideas?" Johnson took a deep breath.

"Nothing yet. There are a couple things, but I can't tell you for security reasons," said Fletcher in his best FBI tone.

Instantly frustrated, Johnson politely asked, "So, what can you tell me? Wait—let me ask you a few questions. Did Mr. Fairchild really work for Senator Henry?"

"Yes. He was his Chief of Staff. I can't tell you much more, Director. We're still trying to piece some things together down here. But I will tell you this, I will be there within twenty-four hours to assist you."

Johnson knew he didn't have much choice in the matter. "That's great. We could use help on this one. Call when you get in town. Wait, wait!" he yelled into the phone. "What kind of poison?"

"It was sarin," Fletcher replied. "Nasty stuff. I'll call you when I get there. And, thank you." Fletcher was gone.

Tim Johnson knew about sarin. During his time in the Middle East, they always had protective clothing and apparatus in case of chemical warfare. Sarin killed instantly, and it was colorless and odorless.

10

Seven p.m. and Parker was in the kitchen cutting up some Tannery Creek chicken. The sweet potatoes were on the stove and salad was already made and in the refrigerator. Keeper and Kali were at his feet, purring and begging for chicken.

The sunset and activity of the day were over. Parker had noticed the two strange vehicles out in front on Mitchell and the one parked in the alley that was blocking traffic from Woodland. He understood he was being watched—hopefully by the good guys.

"Here, Keeper." He dropped a piece of chicken on the floor. "You too, Kali. Here ya go." Another piece hit the polished wood floor.

The knock at the back door startled Parker for a moment; then he remembered no one was coming near his house unless his protection knew about it.

"Moore, it's me." Tim Johnson let himself inside.

"You here for the scotch?"

Keeper and Kali scurried upstairs.

"No. I don't drink anything I can smell a mile away." Johnson walked into the kitchen and sat on a stool.

Parker didn't stop working on the chicken. "Gin's in the freezer. Vermouth and olives down on the bottom shelf." Parker pointed to the refrigerator. "I've got my Lagavulin already."

"Like I said, I can smell it a mile away. Glasses?" Johnson was standing at the door of the freezer reaching in for the gin.

"Here. Have it on the rocks. No fancy martini glasses here." Parker reached up to his right and pulled down a small round water glass.

"No problem. It's a fake martini anyway. I keep the vermouth cap on when I pretend to pour it into the gin." Johnson already had the ice and olives in the glass as he poured in the Bombay gin. London dry was his favorite. "Well, here's to ya, Ernest. Wonder if old Hemingway really drank Bombay martinis at City Park."

"Yes, he did. I was there. In fact, that son of a bitch made fun of my scotch the same way you do." Parker was now marinating the chicken in salt, pepper, olive oil, and fresh basil from Sam's herb garden.

Johnson smiled and sat in the sunroom next to the kitchen where Parker and Sam spent Sunday mornings reading.

"So, Moore, what really happened in all those places when you were a hotshot?" Johnson sipped his gin while holding onto one of Parker's latest charcoal drawings.

"Oh, you know. Stuff." Parker walked into the sunroom, holding his scotch glass in his right hand while flinging the dish towel up over his left shoulder. He sat in the loveseat across from Johnson. "Tim, I heard a lot. I saw a lot. I have no idea what somebody wants now. I have nothing left to hide, keep secret, or want to discover. If I knew anything more, I would tell you." Parker reached over and put an Ella Fitzgerald CD in the stereo.

"You realize someone knew this guy was coming for you—and was protecting you?"

"I figured that out as soon as I saw the bullet hole in the guy's— Hey who was he, anyway?" Parker sat back with both hands holding his drink.

"We don't know yet. We know he's not Fairchild. In fact, the real Mark Fairchild is dead. FBI called and said they found him poisoned two days ago at his home in D.C. Foggy Bottom, to be exact. He did really work for Senator Henry, but that's all I know so far. The Feds are on the prowl and on their way up here.

Parker's phone beeped. He went into the kitchen and looked at it. Sam had sent a text wondering how his day was going. He texted back:

Okay. Miss you. Cats and I cooking chicken.

He returned to his seat in the sunroom. "How many people you got watching the house?"

"I don't have any. Shit, I don't have enough people to watch over you, Parker. They're county and state guys. The paper will talk about a guy having a heart attack on your deck. The case is still under investigation. No one heard anything or saw anything. Guess that's to be expected on a quiet Sunday in Petoskey in the off-season. No tourists. No one up at six. You don't remember hearing anything but the car?" Johnson sipped his gin and waited for an answer.

"Nope. Like I said, I remember the car noise, and that's it."

"Well, I suspect the professional watching you had a silencer too. You got bad enemies and some really badass friends. Remind me not to piss you off." Johnson finished his gin and headed back into the kitchen.

Parker got up and followed him. He went out onto the deck to light the grill then remembered it was still a crime scene. He went into the kitchen and took out a frying pan.

"Hungry?"

"No, but I'll have another," said Johnson as he poured two fingers of gin over his semi-melted ice.

"So, do I make my usual rounds to the clinics tomorrow? Hit the gym? Monday is always Brother Dan night." Parker placed the chicken breast fillets into the frying pan with a little olive oil. The sweet potatoes were done and off to the side.

"I guess so," sighed Johnson. "We'll keep an eye on you, but be prepared for us to come get you or have you come in once the Feds show up."

Parker drank some of his Lagavulin and stared eye level into the fan cover above the stove top. At six foot five, things at eye level were different for Parker. He poked the chicken with some tongs and began thinking about Ramsey and Brooks. He took another drink of the strong Islay scotch and smelled the heavy peat and seaweed aroma as he raised the glass. He remembered the Northern Lights last night and looking over at Bay Harbor with the sensation of security and energy. He wasn't wrong about the outcome. He was safe and suddenly that same energy returned and his mind cleared. He realized the NSA was still watching his back. There must be something he wasn't contacted about. With

Johnson and half the police officers in Emmet County watching him, it might be tough for the good guys to contact him.

"Okay. I'll do my usual thing tomorrow. Call me."

"You got it." Johnson finished his gin and walked toward the door. "I swear Moore, if you're holding out on me, I'll— I'll tell Gurney's and Symons' to stop carrying your scotch. Night."

11

MONDAY ~ OCTOBER 24

Monday morning and Parker found himself face to face with Kali. Keeper was at the bedroom doorway sitting and watching. Kali licked Parker's hand as it stuck out from under the covers.

"Darling, I love it when you do that," he said to the feline as he stayed face down on the pillow. The sun was out, so he figured it had to be after seven thirty. The phone vibrated on the nightstand. He picked it up and brought it down to the pillow so he could see who was calling without lifting his head. It was one of the clinics.

"Hello," Parker said.

"Parker, are you coming to the Petoskey Clinic today?" It was Laura, the new front desk person. She was over six feet tall, dark, and mysterious (to say the least).

"I think so." Parker wasn't fully awake and usually planned leisurely mornings—just because he could. His circadian rhythms were more for a night owl than the early bird. Mornings were always slow.

"Okay. I have some stuff for you to take to another clinic. By the way, what was all the commotion around your house yesterday? Somebody die or something?" Laura laughed as she asked.

Parker lifted his head up and took notice of her question. "Um, no. Just a sick neighbor who came over for some help. How did you know?"

"Oh! I live right down the street from you." Laura was brand-new staff and had only started to work at the clinic two weeks ago. Being from a temp agency, there was never a lot of interviewing or pre-employment screening. She said she was from the Detroit area.

"Laura, you live where?" Parker was now standing at the window of the upstairs bedroom and looking west down Mitchell Street as it disappeared into the downtown district.

"Yes?" Laura talked softly away from the phone. "Hold on, Parker. I have to help someone." She put Parker on hold.

When Laura came back on the line, she said, "Parker, I have to go. But yes, I live right by you." Her tone changed; to Parker it sounded like she was making fun of him. "I've seen you and— is it Sam? Sitting outside on your Adirondacks."

"Oh. Oh, yeah. Um. I'll be in around ten. Okay? See you later." Parker was polite but cautious. His mood tensed and he slowly turned around to see both cats sitting by the doorway watching him.

"What the hell do you guys want, huh? Food? Treats? A piece a me? You both want a piece a me?" Parker was smiling and pretending he was in an alley boxing. As he ran at the cats, they didn't move. Keeper picked up a front paw and licked it. "That's what I thought. Scared the hell outta ya, didn't I?"

Parker walked the short hallway and down the stairs as the hundred-year-old floor boards creaked. He heard the cats tramp down the stairs behind him. Even they made the stairs creak. He had told Sam he'd fix them while she was gone. "Hey, let's eat!" Parker yelled.

He popped open the can of cat food after tuning the radio to Central Michigan University's public radio station. Parker enjoyed listening to NPR. Morning Edition was still on.

He couldn't get the call from Laura out of his head. How many people were new in town that he never thought much about or paid attention to? He looked up at the clock on the microwave over the stove as he dumped cat food onto two small dishes. It was 8:20.

After setting the dishes down for the cats, Parker went into the media room and grabbed the laptop. He turned on the TV and stood there watching CNN for a moment; then turned to walk out. He glanced out the front window and noticed only one car was still out front with one person in the driver's seat. He returned to the back of the house and out the back door, still wearing his gym shorts and a t-shirt and carrying the laptop. The car was gone from the alley, but it didn't mean there wasn't someone around the corner at the bottom of the hill or at the top of the hill at the other end of the alley. Parker walked back into the house.

His phone was vibrating on the cutting board table by the patio door. It was Sam.

"Hey, Doll!" Parker exclaimed.

"Hi, honey. We're getting ready for a morning walk."

It was two hours earlier in Idaho. Six thirty was early for a walk, he thought. "Couldn't sleep?"

"No, I was. Harrison didn't want to; so I figured we'd take an early walk. How's your morning?"

"Good. The cats attacked me, and I had to fight them off." He looked down. They were still licking the plates clean.

"Stop! Sleep was good?"

"Yes, actually. I stayed up and watched the Tigers lose, so we're left with the Red Wings and Lions." Parker was a hockey fanatic. In 1967, he bought a black-and-white RCA TV with his First Communion money just to watch the Red Wings on channel 50 and Hockey Night in Canada on channel 9 out of Windsor. His father loved the Lions, the Chicago Cubs of the NFL, so Parker was always loyal to them as well.

"Well, get a good fix. When I get home, we're back to Sundance movies. I'll call you later tonight. Bye, sweetie." Sam waited.

"Bye, honey. Love you."

They both hit the end button.

Parker was actually surprised how well he did not wanting to alarm Sam. He didn't have any answers and knew she would rush home to nothing that could be solved. His mind returned to his conversation with Laura. He shook his head, let the cats outside, and walked back upstairs to get in the shower.

12

Ramsey was having breakfast in the Rose Room of the Perry Hotel on a bright Monday morning. The room was named after Hiram O. Rose, an 1880's entrepreneur and a friend of Dr. Perry, the dentist who built the hotel in 1899. Ironically, Dr. Perry had the hotel constructed after he treated a patient, and the patient died from complications. It was the good Dr. Perry's escape from the turmoil of the death. Todd Ramsey was, indeed, attempting to keep his own "patient" from a similar fate.

The view across the bay was cloudless, with only a few ripples on Lake Michigan. The fall colors were brilliant in the rising sun behind the dining room. Ramsey was the only one in the room enjoying the scene. The weekend color tourists were gone. He was eating scrambled eggs and bacon and thinking about his partner, John Brooks, and where he must be. The captors said they would kill Brooks if the United States didn't pay them one billion dollars. The informant was missing as well, and the cyber chat about the kidnapping had dried up. *Don't seem like amateurs*, he thought as he shook his head and took another bite.

Small groups and bands of hotshots trying to make a name for themselves, not realizing the listening capability of the NSA and other U.S. organizations, were always eventually caught and killed. This group, however, practiced dead silence. *Why the money and that amount?* he wondered.

He finished the food on his plate and set his fork down with his left hand. Ramsey held his coffee cup with both hands as he stared across the bay. He never felt good about killing, but it had been his job for ten years. After a stint with the Army as a Special Forces sniper, he passed through the Federal Law Enforcement

Training Center in Brunswick, Georgia. At thirty-five, he was single and without much family left in his hometown of Oil City, Pennsylvania. He was a perfect recruit for the NSA, who had fewer field agents than other secret U.S. groups; so, Ramsey's missions were always very specialized. This one was to keep Parker Moore alive until further notice.

He had eliminated one assassin, but the message was clear: there was another. Todd Ramsey had to figure out who it was and not get anyone's suspicions aroused. For whatever reason, his supervisor wanted Moore right where he was. Ramsey couldn't figure out why he wasn't supposed to let Moore know. Hell, why not just grab him and watch him?

The special hangar recently built at Pellston Airport, where Ramsey got his vehicles, was publicly known as a garage for utility vehicles, runway maintenance, and other assorted needs. In reality, it was a well-placed special ops hangar underneath a concrete floor with state-of-the-art communications equipment, an elevator floor with chopper, and resident bunks, plus a whole host of supplies. There was now one in every state and usually in rural places like Pellston. Quiet and strategically located, the hangars were to be used for the rescue of VIPs in a national emergency. Why not just keep Moore there?

Ramsey sipped his coffee and watched his right hand go down with the cup as he returned it to the saucer. The breakfast was just the right way to start what could be a long day. He knew the local departments would be watching Moore; so it was his job to watch and see who might be watching them. A cat-and-mouse spy game reminiscent of the Cold War. It was 9:00 a.m.

Laura moved medical records from one desk to the other as she closed out the files at the clinic in the Crest View Mall on Spring Street. She glanced up at the clock. She had less than five days to finish her work. She told the other staff she was going out back for a cigarette.

Tim Johnson sauntered into his office around 9:15 a.m. He was holding his Roast and Toast travel cup. New ones had just arrived, but he liked the old blue-and-white cups. No new messages on his desk, but the message light on the phone was flashing. He took off his fall trench coat and his sport coat and hung them on the back of the door. He drank some coffee, sat in his chair, and dialed into his voicemail. The only message was from Fletcher. He'd be arriving Tuesday instead of today due to some other information he needed to be sure of prior to discussions in Petoskey.

Johnson erased the message and sat back in his chair. He turned and looked out his office window at the public marina and boat launch. All the slips were empty except for the county sheriff's skiff. The marina office and clubhouse for guests were shut down and locked up. Usually once October rolled around on the northern Great Lakes everyone had their boats out of the water and winterized. The weather was always unpredictable, and the fall winds could be horrific. *Didn't need to be a Gordon Lightfoot fan to know that,* he thought.

He wondered who was out in his community with the ability to kill without conscience? He was just glad that maybe he or she was on his side of the law. And then there was Moore, always the mystery. Johnson was in Lansing the night Moore's ex-wife was killed by a hit-and-run outside the strip club, Omar's. Except for a few questions, the case was closed. The gun that was used to shoot both Moore in the Roast and Toast and the DEA informant was found in the Boyne River by a fisherman and had some of her prints intact. Was it simply karma that someone just happened to run into her that rainy night two years ago? Johnson wondered what Moore was holding back. Even though much of his past life was public, there was enough that wasn't.

Johnson turned his chair around and stood up. His cup was empty; so he headed to the staff kitchen down the hall for a refill.

"So, Parker, this has been fascinating. Thank you. I hope you don't mind if I call you again about finding work here." Catherine stood up and put on her coat. "I'm just going to get a refill and be on my way."

"No problem," Parker said as he stood in the polite manner he was taught. "I'm going to stay here and write." The business meeting at Roast and Toast was ordinary, although the woman was new to town. Throughout their conversation, Parker averted his eyes from Catherine every time someone ventured into the shop that he didn't know. He wasn't afraid; the anxiety was actually exhilarating. And he knew someone in the shop was his shadow, so it became a game to figure out who it was.

"See you soon, Parker. And thanks again." Catherine headed toward the front door as Bob walked in putting on his apron to begin his day helping his staff.

"I should start charging you office rent, Parker." Bob laughed as he walked by.

Parker looked over at the table by the window where he was sitting when he was shot; trying to remember what he could about that day; the feeling of security just before the event and the idyllic life he thought he'd fallen into.

Now, he was sitting at a table next to the menu board working on some poetry while listening to a Bay View resident discuss the closing of his cottage for the winter and all of the intricacies involved, like the plumbing, the windows, the car he leaves up here, and his golf clubs.

Parker was curious about how Catherine found him. He wrote himself a note.

A few late-morning stragglers came in for their first cup of coffee for the day. Meanwhile, soup was out and salads were being prepared for a local catering delivery. It was 11:00 a.m.

13

Tim picked up his phone. "Johnson."

"Hey, Tim. We still don't have much on your John Doe," said Joe Slocumb at the forensic lab.

" 'Not much' means something. What do you have?"

"Well, it was a .32 round reload, untraceable. It was a one-shot kill and definitely by someone who knew what he or she was doing. Fingerprints were matched through Interpol to a Yemen crime committed five years ago that involved kidnapping. His name is Pierre Simon from Corsica. For some reason he was given diplomatic immunity in the Yemen case."

Johnson laughed into the phone. "That's 'not much'? Was he right or left-handed?"

"Left, actually." replied Slocumb.

"Shit, Joe. That's more than I know about my own kids. Boy, this isn't like some local kid doling out meth. I had a suspicion it was going to be big—but I gotta think on this one. The Feds are coming up from D.C. tomorrow. Can I send them over to visit you?"

"No problem, Tim. Call if you can, just so I can stop what I'm doing on Jimmy Hoffa."

"Funny. I know you're good—but let's not go that far. I'll see you tomorrow." Johnson hung up the phone.

After the cigarette break, it was more medical records. Laura looked up and saw Parker coming in from the parking lot.

"Hey, Moore. Right on time, what's up with that?" was Laura's sarcastic welcome as she continued to concentrate on the records she was working on. It was 12:05 p.m.

"Hey, there's always a new start. You said there was stuff for me to take? I'm headed up to Conway and Harbor."

The other clinics were north of Petoskey. One on Conway Road, near the old hamlet of Conway that diminished long ago after the trains and boats stopped connecting the inland waterway between Lake Michigan and Lake Huron. The other clinic was in Harbor Springs, near the schools.

"Yeah. That pile of envelopes and some pool chemicals in that box." Laura was still looking down at her desk. She pointed with her right hand toward the floor by the front counter.

"That's it? Okay. Got it. Well, see you later." Parker picked up everything in one load and started to back his way out of the double-glass doors into the parking lot. "Hey, Laura, did a woman name Catherine Hamilton come in and ask about me some time last week?"

"Yeah. She said she was new in town, doing some contract marketing for a few places in the county and heard you've been around. Why? Is she hot?" Laura looked up from her work and smiled with her head tilted in flirtatious manner.

"What? No. Geez. Thanks." Parker finished backing his way outside.

Laura watched Parker make his way to his car. She noticed two men in a blue Chevy Malibu a few spots behind Parker's Fusion. No one noticed the black Buick sitting on the crest of the hill at the entrance off of US-131.

Parker stopped at each of the clinics. He noticed the Malibu everywhere he went. It wasn't like they were trying to hide from him; they probably wanted everyone else to know they were with Parker wherever he went.

Parker thought about driving through all the commercial

parking lots on his way back to Petoskey just to see if they would finally pull up to him and tell him to stop. Parker was so mesmerized by the Malibu he never saw the black Buick following in a similar shadow.

Parker drove up to St. Francis Church on State Street. It was Monday evening and Brother Dan's was getting ready for the Tuesday rush of people to the food pantry.

"Hey, Parker!" yelled Bill from the kitchen as Parker walked by to hang up his coat in Mary's office.

"What's up tonight, guys? Coffee on?" Parker entered the kitchen where everyone was busy.

"Decaf," Barb said as she measured flour into a mixing bowl. "I'm trying a new cake recipe, so don't leave without trying some."

"Promise." Parker grabbed his coffee and went in and out of the various rooms to help stack groceries, lift heavy boxes, and carry food up and down the stairs. It was his third year volunteering.

"Parker, did you see those two guys out there by your car?" Bill was looking out the front door.

"Yeah, they're okay. They, um, they're looking to buy it. I've been thinking about selling it. You know, one car for Sam and me right now would work." Parker looked over Bill's shoulder to make sure it was the same two guys he'd seen all day. They were just standing by the fence in front of his car by the school playground. Both wore jeans and dark jackets. One was smoking a cigarette.

"Hey, who's that?" Bill noticed a woman walking toward the pantry.

"Wow. That's Laura. Hey, Laura, what are you doing here?" Parker held the door open for her.

The men by his car watched but didn't move. The Buick was off to the far right around the corner of the church and out of Parker's sight. It was empty.

"I'm here to help. They told me you were here every Monday, so I figured I'd come by."

"They who?" Parker asked.

"The people at the clinic. When I said I'd like to volunteer around town, they suggested the pantry; so here I am. Now, what can I do?" Laura hung her jacket on a chair by the front door.

"Hi, I'm Bill. Follow me." Bill took Laura's arm and shuffled her back to the kitchen where there was always work.

As Parker was shutting the door, a man walking by the steps leading to the entry, looked up at Parker. He was wearing a tan Carhartt hunting coat and smoking a cigarette. The man stopped as if he might come in. One of the two men by the fence started to walk toward the stranger, while the one who was smoking, calmly dropped his cigarette and snuffed it out with his foot before getting into the Malibu and starting it.

As if sensing he was being watched, the man in the hunting coat began to slowly head east on State Street past the garages connected to the pantry. The Malibu had backed out of its parking space, while the other officer and Carhartt man passed each other on the sidewalk without incident. The officer got into the Malibu as it pulled alongside him. They then drove to Howard Street, turned the corner, and sat in the first parking spot by the post office. The man in the hunting coat continued to walk toward Waukazoo Street. Parker took a deep breath and sighed. He looked around and went back into the kitchen.

Laura was sitting on a stool next to Barb and Holly putting ingredients for beef stew into small plastic bags. The pantry not only gave out staples like bread, eggs, and canned goods, the staff also put together ingredients for easy meals so families could prepare and make dinner together. It made for late prep nights on Monday, but the one hundred families that showed up on Tuesday always appreciated their efforts.

"Parker, could you hand us more bay leaves over there?" Holly pointed to the spices on the shelf.

"Sure. You've met Laura?" Parker asked the two women.

"We have. She's chipping right in. We've only got a dozen or so more bags to fill, then we're all done." Barb was talking as she was dropping leaves into the bags.

"Well, I'm gonna take off. I'll see you next week. Laura, I'll see you tomorrow."

"Sure will. See ya, Moore." Laura watched Parker as he left the kitchen. She then turned to Barb and smiled.

"Now, mind your ways girl," Holly started. "He's taken. Sam may be gone for a week, but don't go poking around Parker."

Laura continued to smile.

Parker got into his car and drove up the alley to the back of the house. He passed the Carhartt coat man and quickly looked in his rearview mirror to make sure the Malibu was in tow. He pulled into his driveway and the man walked by without looking up. The Malibu slowly followed the man up the alley.

"Hey, are you guys starving?" Parker had Kali at his heels while Keeper watched from the back deck.

"Let's go in and watch a movie." It was 9:00 p.m. Parker followed the felines inside, shut the house up, and closed the shades in the media room. He ate a sandwich and some chips while he watched *The Hunt for Red October*.

The phone started to vibrate. It was Sam.

"Hi, honey. How's things? Today? No big deal …" Parker and Sam talked for five minutes before saying good night.

Out front a white Dodge Challenger was parked. One person lounged in the front seat drinking coffee.

Todd Ramsey made sure Parker was in bed before he returned to his room at the Perry. He hung up his coat and then walked downstairs to the Noggin Room. The Guinness would taste good tonight. As he ordered his beer, he noticed the tan Carhartt coat hanging on the back of an empty bar stool.

14

In a secluded hideaway on the other side of the world—seven thousand one hundred and eighty-one miles and eight time zones away—a detail of Delta Force was gearing up. The five men reviewed the intel, which included detailed floor plans, satellite photos, soundings of wall thickness, and hollow entry points on the roof of their target. The mystery of one guard watching the kidnap victim provided the caution of a possible connected room, alley, or tunnel that allowed for more personnel than they had counted. The setup was either amateurish or purposeful. Regardless, this was to be a quiet operation. No flash. No bang. Minimum show for minimized risk. Air support and a second team waited just outside the city, while a drone quietly flew overhead and a satellite was re-tasked for the timing of the rescue. The well-paid informant said he would leave two side doors loosened on his exit at 4:30 a.m. He would be gone for one hour.

It was 5:00 a.m. and already Tuesday in Yemen. The air was quiet. The five men were in Yemen attire and each had a .45 caliber Heckler & Koch MK 23 with a suppressor and laser-aiming module discreetly hidden under his garments. They also carried .22 caliber close-range pistols and two of the men also carried the reliable MP5SD.

The men split up to walk in three different directions toward a back alley in Yemen's capital city of Sana'a. The cement-walled house was holding an American hostage. The man had been abducted several months ago and, after weeks of surveillance and other covert work, the U.S. was ready to attempt a rescue. There was no American on a publicly known list of captives, but that was not unusual as oftentimes intelligence and military captives were kept off the grid. The Delta Force unit knew who they were assigned to rescue.

A single guard sat in a lone chair in a hallway outside an eight-by-eight room with no windows. He cradled a Kalashnikov in his lap. The chair rested back on two legs against the wall and the guard's head bobbed up and down. His eyes were shut. He had kept this position every night for the last three months; he was bored with the routine. His Yemen-born partner left thirty minutes ago for some food. The U.S. had ignored all requests for ransom—actually had never even communicated with the group about the man in the room. The captive was to be eliminated tomorrow once leaders from the security team arrived.

The Delta Force walked down two alleys that converged on a back street. Since they were separated from each other, nothing seemed odd. They looked like locals walking to the shops. Two even passed each other, but their demeanor and attire brought no attention from the few locals also on the street.

In the blink of an eye, one unit member met up with another in the alley where it backed up to the building. In one motion, he jumped on his partner's back and onto the roof and out of sight. The others ran around to the two entrances, one on each side of the hallway leading to the guard in his chair. At once, both entry doors were down, the old roof door caved in, and a Delta Force member was face to face with John Brooks. Brooks was sitting on a worn mattress on an old metal bed frame. He had a thin wool blanket over his shoulders. John Brooks knew in an instant this was a good guy.

Before the sleeping guard knew what was happening, a round went through his temple. As his body fell from the chair to the right, the AK-47 dropped to the wood floor and bounced away. One Delta Force member moved toward the dead man with his weapon's laser aimed directly on his head. He quickly studied the man and discerned him to be a private mercenary. He was not Middle Eastern.

Two unit members guarded the entrances while John Brooks was quickly dressed in Yemen-style clothing the team had brought. Two Delta Force members walked with Brooks out the left entrance into a different alley. The others split up to meet in an agreed-upon rendezvous point.

In five minutes, it was as if Brooks had never been there.

In Petoskey, it was midnight, Todd Ramsey dozed in bed while CNN played on the TV in his room at the Perry. His partner was already on a plane headed to the island of Diego Garcia in the middle of the Indian Ocean.

15

TUESDAY ~ OCTOBER 25

A windy, rainy, dreary morning and Parker didn't want to get out of bed. He'd had a restless sleep filled with dreams of bad times that added to his dismal attitude. As usual, Kali was on the bed and licking his fingertips.

She meandered by the pillow to stare at him eye to eye. "What? Can't you see I'm pissy? Okay. Okay." Parker slowly pulled back the covers and sat on the side of the bed to look out the window. "How crummy is that, Kali? I'm going to go downstairs and neither one of you is going to want out."

Keeper sat by the doorway. As soon as Parker stood up, Keeper ran downstairs. Kali followed right behind Keeper.

Parker turned on the radio. NPR was airing a discussion about super PACs and the upcoming presidential debates. He smiled and stretched. He took one more look out the window. Lake Michigan was covered in gray mist. Thankfully daylight savings time was ending soon.

As he made his way downstairs, the creak of the floorboards reminded him they needed to be fixed. The kitchen wasn't any brighter and Parker's mood grew worse when he remembered the Feds were going to be in town today.

"Come on, you want out? No? All right. Well, I'll go." Parker went outside on the deck with his gym shorts on, no shirt, and no shoes into the thirty degree rainy morning. He took a deep breath and looked into the rain. His eyes blinked at first; then he was able to keep them open for a bit.

He went back inside and began to grind beans. Just as he finished, his phone vibrated on the counter. It was Johnson.

"Moore? Be here in an hour. Oh, the white van outside is state police. The guys yesterday were county. Just in case you were gonna ask." Johnson clicked off.

Parker never said a word. He put his phone down on the counter and proceeded to make his coffee. While it brewed, he walked to the front door and opened it. Indeed, there was a white panel van. No one was visible, so he suspected their surveillance methods were more subtle now. He walked outside and down the steps to the van on Mitchell.

He knocked on the passenger door and said, "Hey, you guys want some coffee?"

The window came down.

"Ah, Mr. Moore, we're supposed to be watching for your safety not having a public conversation. But, yes. We'd love some. Two black." The plainclothes officer was stern at first, then smiled. It was no secret to anyone that Parker Moore was living with a shadow.

Parker turned and walked through the drizzle and into the house. After he turned, Todd Ramsey drove by in his Buick going east toward downtown.

The man wearing the tan Carhartt jacket was walking up Mitchell toward Parker's house. He was smoking a cigarette as he meandered by the van. His glance was only peripheral, to get a quick look. He continued west toward Lockwood Street and turned the corner going south.

Right behind him was the black Buick. It continued straight on Mitchell, turned right on Kalamazoo, turned right again, and sped west on Michigan to watch the man walk down the alley toward the rear of Parker's house.

Todd Ramsey was convinced this was no coincidence. He wasn't sure if the surveillance team in the van would have notes from the day before about the guy, but Ramsey was on strict orders to not reveal himself until further instruction. Just keep Parker Moore safe and in your sight.

"Senator Henry, we've decided that the Senate Select Committee on Intelligence should keep its meeting for Friday. There's been no publicity and no agenda publicly posted. The group will meet today in the secure room under the National Security Agency." The senator was being briefed on one of his two cell phones.

His interim Chief of Staff, Hal Barnes, a longtime staffer since the Georgia senator's first public office bid in 1964, walked into the room. He noticed a cell phone on the senator's desk that wasn't being used.

"Fine, fine," said Senator Henry as he motioned for Barnes to sit in one of the Queen Anne chairs in a sitting area away from his desk. "I'll make note of that. Thank you, sir." He folded up the phone. "Constituents. You always have to agree, you know."

Hal Barnes watched the senator put the phone in his pocket. Barnes diverted his eyes out the window. The weather was sunny in Washington. Fall colors were peaking and the city was just waking up.

"Any more news on Fairchild?" Senator Henry asked as he grabbed a cup of coffee from the side table and sat down in the comfortable Queen Anne chair next to Barnes.

"Well, yes. That's why I'm curious about this meeting on Saturday." Barnes had closed the door behind him when he walked in. He leaned toward the senator and spoke softly. "Fletcher from the FBI is in Michigan. There seems to be a connection between a death there and Fairchild."

"Really?" The senator sat forward in his chair. It was always hard walking this line with his oldest friend and confidant.

"Seems Fairchild may have been killed by the same people. There have been two other related deaths around the country. The FBI has connected all of them to your committee's investigation of the late Senator Stimson." Barnes was his casual and confident self. Never histrionic in his reactions.

"It's a good thing the FBI is on this. I miss Mark Fairchild." Henry stood and walked away from Barnes. He set his coffee on a table and turned toward the window. He looked out toward the White House and stood with his hands on his hips, thinking.

Unless we do something, the next man to live in that house will be the product of another country with enough money to buy souls, produce any media, and have influence over our way of life by controlling a super PAC. *That guy walking along the Mall doesn't have a clue*, he thought to himself

The senator ran his right hand through his thinning hair and looked down. Friday. Let's hope we can get our men here and keep our heads down. If only Stimson were here. I hope he knows we haven't dropped the ball. Senator Henry turned toward Barnes. "Thanks, Hal. Thanks very much for the update."

Barnes nodded and left the room. After he shut the senator's door, he was immediately on his cell phone. It was 9:00 a.m.

Deep under NSA headquarters in Fort Meade, Maryland, five people sat at the round table.

"What's the latest?" asked the only female in the room.

"Two have died suspiciously—or should we just say have been killed? The other is still alive and where he's supposed to be," noted the gentleman to her right.

"So, why not bring him in?" asked a man from across the table.

"He's bait. We need the insider and whoever is at the other end of the money." said the gentleman who first spoke.

The woman leaned forward with her elbows on the glass table and looked around. "Do we still go public?"

"Friday," said Senator Henry as he walked into the room. He took a seat at the small table.

"Has our information been leaked that it might be Saturday?" asked the woman.

"Yes," answered Henry. "How much money has passed through?"

"One billion so far, over five years," said Grant Holloway, the Director of the NSA. He was a forty-year veteran of public service and the President's handpicked man.

Senator Henry sat back in his chair. The woman got out of hers. The position she held in the previous administration prepared her for what she was hearing, but how to fix it was becoming a far greater task than she had ever imagined.

"Anything more from our man in Yemen?" she asked.

"No. He's still being debriefed by State in Diego Garcia. We'll debrief him here on Thursday."

"All right then," the woman said, sitting back down. "Let's call it a day. We'll meet again on Friday, unless you hear otherwise. Mr. Attorney General, I hope you know what you're doing," she said as she looked to her left.

"We'll use the public hearing to put all the pieces together and make our case," he said as he looked at her.

"Good day, gentlemen." She remained sitting while the others walked out the door, down the hall, and passed the guards by the elevator. She wondered how deep this was going to get and who the casualties would be.

16

"Look, Agent Fletcher, I've told you all I know. I never met Fairchild. I spoke with Senator Stimson and we discussed health care. I left his office and went back to Alaska." Parker was sitting at a rectangular table in a small interview room at the Petoskey Public Safety office. It was 12:30 p.m. He wasn't going to tell Fletcher anything.

Tim Johnson sat in a similar metal chair with green padding next to Parker. His tie was loose at the knot, and he was eating a roast beef sandwich from Julienne Tomatoes.

"Don't you think we've been over this enough, Fletcher?" Johnson said as he chewed his latest bite.

"No. Moore has a pretty public background, but he's not telling us everything." Agent Fletcher paced behind the two men. "What we know is that Stimson's plane was full of his cronies and other business people he was working with and for. The NTSB has never publicly stated the true cause of the crash, except to say pilot error, at our request. The fact that some of his staff took positions with Senator Henry in Georgia, and now Fairchild being poisoned, is not coincidence. Oh, and nothing points to suicide."

Parker was never sure how much the FBI knew about his work with NSA. He figured if the FBI was asking him these questions, they didn't know anything.

"And how does a guy from Corsica posing as Mark Fairchild and carrying an assassin's weapon end up dead on his deck?!" Fletcher bellowed. After three hours of questioning, he was getting exasperated.

Parker just sat and said nothing. Fletcher continued to drone.

"Okay. We're not getting anywhere. Unless you're here with some kind of directive to take over the case, I think we're done for now." Johnson had finished his sandwich and forcefully wiped his mouth with a napkin. "We have Moore under surveillance. We know he didn't do it. We are looking into every lead we have."

"Leads? Do you have any?" Fletcher sat down across the table.

"Well, we know where the victim was from, why he was here, and that he was left-handed." Johnson seemed proud of his forensics man in Gaylord. "Other than that, nothing," Johnson replied as he looked into Agent Fletcher's eyes. "We know Moore's background and we are checking old acquaintances and any enemies for motives, of which there are many." Johnson looked at Parker with a stern grin. "And we are checking around town for any newcomers, since most tourists have left for the season. We'll ask around at the restaurants and hotels to see if anyone has seen people who don't fit the mold of the few seniors who drive up here to look at the fall colors. And, you already know we have cooperation from both state and county law enforcement. Unless we lock him up, there's not much more we can do with Mr. Moore."

"Fair enough. Let's go to Gaylord to see the body; then I'll head back to D.C." Fletcher grabbed his suit coat off the back of the chair and put it on.

Tim Johnson and Jack Fletcher left the interview room while Parker remained sitting. He was thinking about the woman with the clipboard in Stimson's office. "Moore? You coming?" called Johnson from the hallway. "Come on. The county guys aren't busy enough." Johnson made a broad sweeping motion with his left arm to indicate to Moore that he needed to get up. It was after 1:30 p.m.

Todd Ramsey received nothing from headquarters that indicated anything was amiss in Petoskey. So, while Parker was safely being interviewed, Ramsey drove around Parker's neighborhood; surveyed his house, the alley and street; and went into any establishment Parker frequented. Ramsey's cover as an author researching a book seemed to be working. Wherever he went, people were friendly and willing to offer him information. Ramsey found himself sitting at the end of the bar in front of the picture of Ernest Hemingway at the City Park Grill. Brian was bartending.

"Excuse me … I'm in town writing a book about the Great Lakes …"

Brian interrupted, "Really? Here's my card." Brian gave Ramsey a business card acknowledging his membership and presidency of the local chapter of Trout Unlimited.

"Well, then. You could probably help," Ramsey said as he slipped the card into his shirt pocket. "But, actually, I wondered if you knew Parker Moore. He's supposed to meet me here later."

"Oh, yeah. We just did a clean-up of the Bear River earlier this month. He comes in all the time with Henry. They usually sit over there at the table by the window." Brian pointed to the raised stage area by the north window.

"Henry?" Ramsey inquired.

"Yes. They've been coming in for over a year."

"Great, great. So, how about a Maker's Mark, straight?"

"You got it." Brian turned and grabbed the bottle between the Crown Royal and Jameson.

Ramsey was contemplating his next venue. He'd been all over town mentioning Parker's name, but no nuances surfaced that indicated something new or someone that might want to kill him. It was now after 3:00 p.m.

The back tables at Jolly's Cookies and Café on Mitchell Street were reserved for Internet geeks, but this afternoon only one person wearing headphones sat there. This area was not visible from the street. One couple looked like they were having a grand old time. They talked, laughed, and looked around while drinking coffee at a table by the rear door. In between their acting, the discussion was serious.

"You only have two more days," said the man. He was in his thirties and wore blue jeans and a light blue denim Carhartt shirt.

"*We* actually have three days. Don't lay this on me. He's watched 24/7. What the hell am I supposed to do?" She was in her twenties and wore a knee-length dress and black boots that provided the look of a typical professional woman off of work early. She never stopped smiling while she talked.

"You're the journeyman professional. I'm just the apprentice here. The weather doesn't help. Have you planned something different than poison?" He laughed as he asked the question.

"Yes. Never use the same method twice in a row or too close to the last. It won't be pretty, and you and I will have to be in sight distance."

"I don't care what it is. The money's been wired to the account already. If not him, it's going to be us next." The laughter stopped since the only person near them had left. "The first two seemed easy."

"Apparently they didn't count on this one having a shadow. He's never alone, anywhere. Don't forget, it's not the ones we can see we have to worry about." She ended her sentence with her face only about a foot from his.

A young man in a gray hoodie sauntered to the back to use the Wi-Fi.

"Tomorrow. I'll stay invisible, unless I get a good chance." He got up and left out the back door.

She sat momentarily and finished her coffee. One leg crossed over the other as she stared at the pictures of the owner on the wall in front of her. She tipped the cup all the way toward her face and mouth for the last drop; then bused the table.

"Thanks again," she said, waving to the barista as she walked out the front door. She climbed into her white Audi and drove off.

"Henry, look. It's after four and I have one more clinic to visit. After I hit the gym, I'll come get you around six? How's that?" Parker was driving south from Conway and talking about Tuesday bowling night. He looked in his rearview mirror. The blue Malibu was back.

Parker pulled into the clinic in Harbor Springs. He got out and nodded at the Malibu as it backed into a parking spot at the far northwest corner of the lot. When he entered the door, Laura was waiting with a note.

"Hey, Moore. Some guy was calling about a ski team needing a dry land workout prior to the season. Here's his number."

"Thanks, Laura. Hey, who's the new therapist?" Parker had noticed a new face at the Petoskey clinic but hadn't had time to introduce himself.

"Rocco. Rocco Stern. Is that a name or what? He just came on from the same temp agency I did. Nobody knows anything about him. I do know he has a wife, Jessica, and they live on Mitchell up from you. I guess he's a big hunter." Laura watched her computer screen processing patient billings as she talked.

"Really? What the hell? Is everybody moving onto Mitchell?" Parker set his briefcase on the floor and grabbed the stool to sit at the other computer.

After an hour, Parker was done. Laura was still finishing her billing.

"Well, that was exciting. You gonna be long?" Parker stood and stretched. He had put the Fletcher interview out of his mind. He knew he was safe under the watchful eyes of the Malibu and that somewhere the NSA lurked behind it. It was a strange sense of security that no one else in Petoskey or Harbor Springs probably enjoyed. As he put on his coat to leave, he also realized there was a reason for all of this to be happening. Why didn't he know what it was? He had a sudden sense of being alone, even with the shadows. "See ya tomorrow?" he asked Laura as he walked around the counter and toward the door.

"Probably. I don't know where I'll be." She didn't look up until Parker was out the door. She noticed the Malibu; then slowly looked back at the computer screen. It was 5:15 p.m.

17

Parker had picked up Henry. They walked into Northern Lights Recreation. Joe and Ed were behind the counter.

"Yo, Parker. This guy came in earlier asking about you. Didn't leave a number or anything, only went on about some book he was writing." Joe punched numbers into the computer to get the lane set up. Ed grabbed Henry's credit card to pay for the two games they bowled every Tuesday.

"Really? I suspect it's the Superior trip he heard about." Parker feigned the idea of his circumnavigation for 2014, but a relaxed affect came over him. It *was* NSA. They'd track his phone and know everywhere he went, so they could check the same places. The mystery of Stimson snitching wouldn't leave his mind. And this wouldn't be Brooks' way. Brooks would already be in Parker's face if he was in town. *That* was his way. Ramsey? Maybe. Parker wondered what the hell was going on. His phone vibrated as he opened the locker to grab his bowling ball and shoes.

"Sam? How are you? Where the hell have you been?"

"I'm holding Harrison. We've been busy." Sam was barely audible as she held the phone up to her ear with her shoulder. "Where the hell have you been?"

"Me too; busy I mean. Nothing new though. Same old same old." Parker stopped reaching for the bowling ball and stood to talk into the phone. He was smiling.

"I missed you today. Is everything all right? Usually you're texting me every hour."

"Yes. I'm good. How's Idaho?"

They talked for a short while; Parker noticed Rocco walking toward him.

"Honey? Let me call you back later." He ended the call. "Rocco, hi, I'm Parker."

"I know. I've heard all about you. Just up with my wife to throw a couple games." Rocco turned and pointed to a woman lacing up her shoes on lane 15, right next to Henry on lane 16. Rocco was wearing a tan Carhartt coat.

The guys from the Malibu drank a beer at the counter while watching Parker and Henry bowl two games. Two unseen county deputies ran to their car as Parker and Henry left the building. As they drove off it was 9:00 p.m. Rocco was still inside bowling.

Todd Ramsey sat in his gray Buick at the very rear of the bowling alley parking lot. The new car wasn't as comfortable as the black Lacrosse. He waited until the Malibu left after Moore's Fusion. He yawned as he made his way south on M-119 following both cars.

There were three new people in Parker's life, and Ramsey was only one man. There might be a need to bring the local department in on his part of the case just to make sure Parker remained safe. Ramsey made sure Parker dropped Henry off and was back home before he stopped tailing him. The white van was on Mitchell Street and a brown van was on Woodland at the bottom of the alley. Ramsey headed down to the Palette Bistro instead of the Noggin Room as he continued to look everywhere Parker frequented.

John Brooks was in a hospital gown and cold. He was still trying to shake off his three months of captivity. He had finished a long interview session with two people from the State Department and was waiting in a small, white, stark room with metal trays of instruments, a sink, and metal counter for the base physician to give him a physical.

"Agent Brooks?" The flight surgeon walked into the room and closed the door behind him.

"Yes. John Brooks."

"Sounds like you've had quite an experience. All your labs look good. Any injuries or issues from the events over the last several months?" The physician was looking at papers in a manila folder with his glasses down on his nose. He only looked up to talk. The stool he sat on was directly in front of the examining table Brooks sat on with his legs hanging over the end.

"Actually, no. I am surprised I'm alive. I thought they'd kill me at some point. It's as if they knew they weren't going to kill me. A ploy or a diversion."

"Well, lucky you then. Let's take a look." The physician started the exam by listening to Brooks' heart and lungs. He visually looked the agent over as he probed and prodded. "Everything looks and sounds good. Little hungry, I suspect."

"Yes. That I am."

"Okay. You're good to go. There's a detail waiting outside to get you to D.C. by way of Ramstein. Good luck, Agent Brooks. Hopefully we don't see you again." The physician smiled and held his hand out to shake. He never asked questions of the people he encountered at Diego Garcia. As a matter of fact, that was a direct order he heard often from the base commander.

"Thank you, sir." Brooks shook the right hand of the physician, who departed the room. After Brooks dressed into civilian clothes, he was met by two uniformed Air Force Special Ops Sergeants. He felt safe with these two men. He walked down the hall, confident and in a hurry to tell somebody the real story instead of the dribble he fed to the State Department boys.

It was already Wednesday in the Indian Ocean.

18

"Parker Moore? Oh yeah, he comes in once in a while. His artwork is upstairs. Something I can get for you?" Joe wasn't very busy bartending, but he was busy watching the Red Wings pound the Anaheim Ducks. It was a typical fall weeknight at the Palette. Aleece was taking care of a few customers at the high-tables around the front of the restaurant, and Sean, one of the servers, was barking an order back to the kitchen as he leaned against the bar. The open kitchen was just to the right and behind the bar.

"Yeah. Um, let's see ... a Huma-Lupa-Licious." Todd Ramsey liked his beers, but had no idea what the local breweries offered. He didn't want to be too touristy even though his cover was researching a book. He figured he'd take what he got in the glass and enjoy it.

"There ya are. Hey, you're the guy writing the book on the Great Lakes, eh? So you know about Parker and his kayak?" Joe was excited to talk to anybody who'd listen.

Patrick, one of the owners, sauntered over to listen. "If you're looking for Parker Moore, he's probably at home. His nights end early unless he's sitting at the bar writing.

Ramsey didn't hear anything after Joe said he knew who Ramsey was. He didn't hear a word Patrick said either. This revelation meant even the bad guys in town might soon know about Ramsey's presence. "Kayak? Oh, yeah. The kayak. Sure. What did you say about writing?" He took a long draw of the beer and turned toward Patrick. The IPA was intensely hoppy and quenching. He just listened to Joe and thought about what to do next. The hardest part about small towns is how fast information travels. Sometimes that's a purposeful tool, but Ramsey walked a fine line between being visible and too visible.

"Oh, that some nights Parker comes in late at night to write. Not sure what, but he's always busy doing it. Enjoy your beer." Patrick walked over to the entrance to seat a couple just arriving for a nightcap.

It was 11:27 p.m.

Parker was dozing off while reading in bed. Beethoven's *Moonlight Sonata* played softly on the CD player. He reached over and turned off the lamp on the nightstand.

As he rolled over, he heard the cats run upstairs and under the bed. The air was still. Parker's eyes were wide open and he did not move. He was lying on his side, facing the west wall of the bedroom. He slowly reached down and gripped his old Maglite police flashlight. The floor at the bottom of the stairs creaked. With the cats under the bed, no one else was around to cause the sound. Another creak. The first step board he was supposed to fix. There was a long pause.

Parker quickly and quietly turned from his right side to his left so he faced the door. He sat up and took two soft leaps to crouch next to Sam's black dresser near the entry to the room. The flashlight was at his side in his right hand.

The silence was long.

Parker didn't move.

There were five soft steps and a creak at the top board near the bathroom. The other board Parker was supposed to fix while Sam was gone. Parker was breathing faster. Every muscle was tense, and he was angry. *This has got to stop*, he thought.

The doorway was situated in such a way that you had to come into the room to see the bed in the northwest corner. The steps stopped. Four suppressed shots rang from a gun he saw about five feet above the floor. The bullets hit the bed by the headboard and into the mattress. Parker was holding his breath. His heart pounded in his ears. The arm connected to the gun walked through the door, soon followed by the rest of the body.

In one motion Parker stood up tall and forcefully swung his right arm downward with the four D-battery black flashlight in his hand. He hit the person directly on top of the head with the butt end of the light. The body slumped to the floor. The automatic weapon hit the floor and discharged twice, hitting the window.

As the glass shattered outside, the officer in the white van jumped out with his weapon drawn and ran up to the front door. He was on his radio calling for backup as he launched his shoulder against the front door. He could already hear sirens.

"Moore!" he yelled as he entered the living room. With his weapon out he scanned the dark.

"I'm okay. I'm up here, in the bedroom. But this guy might be dead." Parker felt the carotid artery of the man lying face down in his bedroom.

Pete Stuart was a twenty-year state police veteran. He'd never had to shoot anyone before, but his training and experience told him to walk upstairs with his weapon guided by his eyes and covering any open space as it came into view.

"I'm going to turn on the hallway light; so don't flip out." Parker reached the switch.

Stuart was walking up the stairs almost backwards. With the light on, Stuart saw Parker was alive. He continued up the stairs with his weapon pointed at the body on the floor.

"You all right?" he asked Moore. Stuart could hear the sounds of his fellow shadows. Other officers were arriving and the brown van on Woodland was already in the back driveway. "Moore's okay. One down." Stuart said into the collar mic on his jacket. "How the hell did he get in?"

"Have no idea." Parker, dressed in his gym shorts and a GVSU t-shirt, slid his back down the bedroom wall until his butt hit the floor. He noticed blood on the flashlight. "Shit."

There was noise all over the house. Four other men were upstairs; some still had weapons drawn. One held a shotgun at his side. Stuart was on his cell phone.

"Director, Parker Moore had an intruder. He's safe."

"Give me ten. Make sure we lock down the block," said Tim Johnson as he reached for his clothes.

Parker's phone vibrated on the nightstand. It was a text from Sam:

Sweet dreams! Love you.

19

Todd Ramsey was sitting at the corner of the bar watching the game. Looking out the window, he had seen the patrol car parked behind Papa Lou's bar waiting for the drunks to come out. Suddenly the patrol car flipped its flashers on and flew out of the lot, driving over the curb.

"Holy mother f—" Ramsey was out of the Palette in a flash. He knew something was wrong.

He jumped in the gray Buick, turned it around on Bay Street, and headed toward Parker's house. He slowed when he saw flashers and emergency cars everywhere. Men were coming and going from the house. Neighbors' lights were on. This wasn't low profile.

A police officer directed Ramsey to drive around the left side of the boulevard since there was no traffic coming the other way. Ramsey drove around as directed and looked up to the second floor of Parker's house and wondered what had happened. He turned left onto Summit since the right turn onto Lockwood was blocked by an unmarked, then he drove around onto Lake Street and parked. Ramsey got out of his car and walked back around toward Parker's to watch from behind some bushes. He had a scope in his hand.

She watched from the window of the house. No lights were on. A cell phone was at the ready in her hand.

It was now after 1:00 a.m. Tim Johnson walked into the house to find Parker sitting at the dining room table sipping out of a crystal scotch glass.

"You're gonna become an alcoholic, Moore," he said as he stood ready to go upstairs.

"Yeah, well, it beats having people keep trying to kill you." Parker's eyes never left the glass as he held it in both hands swirling the Lagavulin ever so slowly. He dipped his nose into the glass and took a deep breath. "Glad you're here, Tim. I'm about at the end of my rope—again." Parker forced a smile.

"Sit tight. I'll be right back." Johnson ran up the stairs. There was an outline where the body used to be. "What do we have?" he asked as he bent down on one knee for a closer look. He saw the blood pooled on the wood floor.

"We had the guy rushed over to Northern. He was still alive, but he had quite a gash in his head. Moore dealt him a pretty heavy blow." Pete Stuart was leaning on the black dresser. Pictures were still being taken around the room. Fingerprints were also being processed, even though the shooter was wearing gloves. The Maglite lay on the floor right where Parker dropped it when he slid down the wall. Suddenly the cats peered out from under the bed and scurried downstairs.

"Think they saw anything?" Johnson smiled as he turned and watched them run down the stairs.

Stuart just laughed and shook his head.

"Okay. We about done here, everyone?" Johnson looked the part in his tan trench coat. All he needed was a cigar and a fedora for a 1950's detective movie.

"Yup. Just taking the last print off the light," said one of the county detectives.

"Who's at the hospital with our perp?" Johnson asked.

"Your two guys. One in the rescue and the other drove the van." Stuart was starting out of the room.

Johnson followed. "Good. I'll sit with Moore here, for a while. Get everybody out of the neighborhood. Pretty soon *The New York Times* will be here," Johnson said in jest.

"Too late, Director," said Stuart when he saw Harvey Snow,

the senior staff writer for the *Petoskey News and Review*, standing in the living room.

Johnson looked up.

"Shit," he said quietly. "Harv, nothing now. Give me a while and I'll call you. I promise."

"Come on, Tim. What the hell's going on? I got a deadline in the morning; you know that," said Snow with his best impression of a street-smart reporter. Actually, the most excitement he'd ever had was when Parker was shot at the Roast and Toast two years ago. Since then, it'd been small town scandal and social events.

"Later," was Johnson's stern reply. "Outta here." He motioned his head toward the door as he stood with his hands in the pockets of his trench coat.

Harvey Snow swore under his breath and left the house. The rest of the deputies and officers also departed. In a few minutes, all was quiet.

"I don't know yet. I'll call you back." She shut off the phone. She couldn't tell from her window who had been carried into the ambulance and rushed to the hospital.

Ramsey walked around the corner onto Mitchell Street when he saw all the vehicles leave. The neighbors had turned off their lights and no one was on the street. He made his way just west of Moore's house and crossed over to the south side of Mitchell for a better view. He could see lights on the first floor. He had to cross back over to the north side to use his scope to see into the front door and window.

He took a deep breath when he saw Parker sitting at the dining room table talking. Johnson had his back to the door. Ramsey knew he had to make a field decision. Later in the day, he'd pay Johnson a visit. Ramsey started back to his car.

She stood quietly, watching the dark figure cross back and forth across the street. She lost sight of the figure once it went around the corner from her window. She sat back down on the bed and thought about Thursday.

"Boy, I've felt so secure with you guys around—but this is not good. I never saw this one coming." Parker was still looking at his glass, even though it was empty.

"I'm sorry, Parker. We've been following you everywhere. I suspect he came in when we were all down at City Hall with the Feds. I'll have to call Fletcher and tell him." Johnson was visibly concerned. He rested his folded arms on the table in front of him. His head was bent as he looked into Parker's face.

"Yeah, that'll help," Parker replied facetiously. "Do you believe this crap? Worst of all, I don't know why it's happening. It was all supposed to be over."

"Parker, it is what it is—and it's not over. I'm as frustrated as you are. This small town's not used to this. We have some guy from Corsica or Yemen a few days ago—and now this. Fletcher's right. You obviously aren't telling everything. You ready now?" Johnson poured himself a scotch.

"I thought you hated that stuff?" Parker said.

"Me, too. But, it's time we talked."

It was 2:52 a.m.

20

WEDNESDAY ~ OCTOBER 26

It was evening in Dubai, United Arab Emirates. The quiet lounge was softly lit and Frederic Chopin's *Preludes* played on hidden speakers. Strategically placed leather chairs and sofas offered a comfortable group setting. The bar behind the largest sofa was stocked with everything from milk to the finest wines and spirits. Windows on the opposite side of the bar provided a view of the top of the building and more than twenty miles beyond. A lone server walked amongst the guests and served a martini to a suited gentleman entertaining a young woman with long black hair wearing a short dress, pearl necklace, and high-heeled pumps. She sipped vodka on the rocks.

In another corner four men and two women quietly discussed the worldwide oil markets and profits. Oil was now just over one hundred dollars a barrel. One of the men said something about Venezuela and the rest of the group laughed.

"Ladies. Gentlemen. Shall we?" A tall man with a British accent stood by one of the leather chairs in the group area. He looked around the room, held up his drink, and motioned for the others to join him.

"So, is everyone comfortable?" he asked as everyone found their seats. They nodded and in a mock toast, held up their drinks to say yes. "Good. Let us begin."

At Northern Michigan Community Hospital, the man with the cracked skull laid in a bed in ICU guarded by three patrolmen. One inside the room; two outside. Nurses, aides, and clerks made their way around the unit in their normal routine. Respiratory therapists came to check the equipment. The man was on life support. The heart monitor showed a regular rhythm, and the rest of his vital signs were also stable.

Tim Johnson walked into the room with Jack Fletcher, who had cancelled his flight to D.C. as soon as Johnson called him about Moore's close call.

The staff hospitalist followed them in. "He's probably going to be okay, but he's very concussed."

"Probably not going to talk?" Fletcher asked.

The doctor looked at Johnson. "Dr. Richland, this is Jack Fletcher, with the FBI."

"Pleasure." They nodded at each other as Richland responded. "Talk? I don't know when he'll wake up."

"I assume we've printed him. Any ID or anything?" Fletcher stared at the man in the bed. The constant low beep of the monitors continued. The ventilator pumped and his chest went up and down in a slow steady motion.

"Nothing so far. Prints didn't give us anything yet. Gun was bigger. An MK23 .45 and lasered." Johnson, now in his suit, sat in the chair at the end of the bed. The patrolman asked permission to leave to get some coffee. Johnson held up three fingers.

"Just black for me, thanks," Fletcher said. "Where's Moore?"

"Sleeping. It was a long night. I told him you'd be here. I figure we'll give him till dinnertime. And yes, we have someone inside and outside his house."

Fletcher nodded and leaned against the windowed wall. The curtains were drawn and the door was shut. The fatigue was evident on Tim Johnson's face. He sat slumped in the chair one leg out and one bent at the knee. The two men stared at a mystery—although now the Director of Public Safety had a better idea why this was happening. Parker Moore told him everything.

At 11:30 a.m. Todd Ramsey sat outside a clinic in the Crest View Mall. He was parked in the southwest corner of the lot in front of Kmart. He watched people coming and going through his scope.

═══

"Ah, Rocco. Where did you get that coat? I was looking for one just like it for my boyfriend. He's up here with me, getting ready for hunting season." Laura was standing at the counter. Rocco was just walking by on his way outside for lunch.

"It was really strange. I was working at the Conway Clinic when this guy came in for a free assessment. He kept asking a lot of questions about people who worked here and for the City of Petoskey." Rocco leaned over with his elbows on the front counter. "He said he was from out of town, and heading back to Florida. I told him I was new in the area and was the wrong person to ask. Next thing I know, he says thanks. For what, I'm not sure. He said he had knee pain, but his strength and flexion were fine." Rocco stared behind Laura with a distant look in his eyes. He brought his gaze back to Laura. "So, anyways, he says he won't need the coat and wants me to have it for giving him the assessment. After I told him I didn't like to accept gifts from patients, he left without saying anything and I saw that the coat was left on the hook by the door. Since it was a free assessment, the only information I got out of him was his name: John Smith."

"And?" Laura hadn't moved.

"So, at the end of the day, I took the coat. I had no phone number for him, and I was cold. Not used to this weather. It was strange. Anyway, see ya after lunch." Rocco gave a short wave and headed out the door.

Laura's phone rang from an internal line. "Yes, this is Laura?"

═══

Ramsey spotted the tan Carhartt as it exited the clinic and found its way into a silver minivan. The coat was familiar, but the guy in it was a different build and balding, unlike the man Ramsey had seen in Parker's neighborhood. The minivan didn't make sense either. Then, he smiled. *I sit in an old gray LeSabre while the suspect drives away in a minivan; now that would not be the case in a Bourne or Bond movie*, he thought.

"As we move forward, we believe our interests will soon be totally protected again. Two of the difficulties have been silenced, and one is being handled as we speak." The tall British gentleman sat with his legs crossed and carefully brushed lint from the knee of his navy blue slacks. His jacket was open and spread perfectly around his chest and waist, and a white shirt, solid red tie, and black wing-tip shoes completed his wardrobe. His other hand rested across the top of the sofa and held Tanqueray on the rocks.

"Excuse me, but are we sure it's being handled? We've been misled before," said the woman to his left who was from Norway.

"I assure you, we have multiple assets working around the clock," answered a man in a black sport coat, black turtleneck, and tan pants. He was from the United States.

"And, we appreciate the work from Gulf Coast Oil," noted the Brit.

Gulf Coast Oil had just made ten billion dollars in profit the last quarter. Their Houston, Texas, office was actually located in the suburb called Sugar Land. As one of the safest cities in America, according to FBI crime statistics, and the second largest economic growth area in the Houston environs, Sugar Land was a reputable community by anyone's standards—and wealthy. The intention was to maintain the wealth, and Jim Reegan, CEO of Gulf Coast Oil, was champion of that cause.

"You're welcome." Reegan stood up and continued talking as

he made his way to the bar; the server already making him another martini. "We have information that there will be a meeting held this Saturday in Washington that could disturb our goals. The security detail handling the mission across the Khali and the Peninsula in Yemen has faltered; therefore, the concentration on our last difficulty has been increased. I've been assured the best possible contract is in place." He stood by the back of the long sofa and looked down at the Brit as he talked.

"Fine. Right. So, let us proceed to the next order of business." The British accent, eloquent in its delivery, was hesitant for a moment. Sir Edward Framingham adjusted his tie and set his drink on the table in front of him. As President, CEO, and prime shareholder of North Channel Petroleum, his company had become responsible for much of the world's oil supply, including everything from the bolts used for the equipment to the survey companies looking for new fields. Their total capital was three hundred and fifty billion dollars. The group he was leading had well over one trillion dollars in assets.

"Excuse me, if I may," said a gentleman in Saudi attire. "Before we leave this point, is this the difficulty that began a few years ago?"

"Yes," answered Reegan as he made his way back to his seat. He sipped his martini and answered, "This began with a meeting in Juneau, where we had assets working to make our situation and goals clear. There was a discussion that we later learned had been recorded." He looked toward the distinguished Sir Edward with a terse smile.

"Yes, that was an unfortunate mistake. No—shall we say *encounter*? Albeit a profitable visit, it was an unfortunate happening." He stared back at his fellow executive. "Now, shall we?"

Mr. Reegan hoisted his martini glass and nodded.

It was the softest part of the year in Dubai. October and early November saw a chilling of the air at night that was most comfortable for those not used to the heat. The only complaint from the new high-rises was the fog that formed as the air cooled sooner than the water. The fog sheltered the night view of the participants, and also anyone looking up at the glass skyscraper.

It was 6:30 p.m. in Germany as John Brooks awaited his flight from Ramstein Air Base. He'd been thinking about the information he had acquired about his Yemen captivity and the connection to money in a Swiss bank. He knew three lives back in the States were in danger and he also knew who the leak was in the Super PAC.

His plan was to fly home and meet with his field supervisor and Senator Henry on Thursday afternoon. The State Department and FBI were still swinging at shadows.

21

The phone vibrated on Parker's nightstand. He reached out from under the covers.

Where are you? I'll be home in three days! Miss you.

Parker closed the phone and looked at the time. 2:13 p.m. He pulled back the covers and sat on the edge of the bed. As he ran his hands through his hair, he realized how long it was getting. He had a habit of letting it grow until Sam would say that he wasn't still in the 1970s. It was more out of laziness.

He walked to the bathroom, then stopped and looked downstairs. "Stuart? You there?"

"I'm here. You awake or just dreamin'?" Stuart was sitting in the dayroom reading a *National Geographic* and listening to the radio. "Moore, you have some boring-ass magazines. *Wine Spectator. National Geographic. The Atlantic.* Lah-de-dah."

"Yeah? Well, the centerfolds are Nobel winners in lingerie. Don't get too excited." Parker shut the door and turned on the shower. As the water ran, he kept sticking his hand in the flow to see if the temperature was warming. He hated the shower in the morning, even if it was technically now afternoon.

Last night was still fresh in his mind. Not so much the man and the flashlight or even the bullets, but the fact that he bared his soul about his past to Tim Johnson. He trusted Tim and knew he had his best interests in mind; so out it came. Michigan, Chicago, Alaska, Washington D.C., the politics, the unions, the money—everything just flowed like he'd wanted to tell somebody for years. The part about his ex-wife getting killed was easier to tell. The abusive marriage was passé. The life he'd found the last four years in Harbor Springs and Petoskey was nirvana. If

Ramsey was around, good. If Stimson ratted him out, well, he wasn't sure about that. In any case, he figured it was time someone in town knew his whole story. It was a relief. His long sleep was proof of that.

He finished the shower and walked into his dressing room. He was so preoccupied he forgot to shave. If Ramsey was out there, maybe he was trying to stay out of the milieu of the everyday routine in Parker's life. It's not like the NSA field agent wanted to be on the side of the milk carton in Petoskey. As Parker dressed, he stopped. The City Park Grill. Tonight. The tunnel. I'll shake everybody and see if Ramsey's out there.

"Moore? Hurry up. We got places to go." It was Johnson downstairs with Fletcher in tow.

"I'm comin'. I'm comin'." Parker buttoned his shirt; then picked up his phone and started to return calls as he came down the stairs.

"Come on. We're going over to City Hall." Johnson was motioning to the front door.

Parker waved at him as he listened to voicemails. The first was a client wanting to meet at 1:00 p.m. The second was a call from Sam. The third was a request from Laura for a ride to work. The final call was from Rocco's wife inviting Parker over for dinner on Thursday.

"Ramsey, we have had three calls of interest from your area since Saturday night. One from an area in Bay Harbor and the other two from Mitchell Street near our man." It was Ramsey's field supervisor, John Mansfield, in Fort Meade, Maryland.

"Okay. And …?" Ramsey pulled his car into the city parking lot behind Center City Gym and Mitchell's Pub.

"They all went to a company in Sugar Land, Texas, called Gulf Coast Oil. The phones are owned by the same company." The supervisor was businesslike. No hyperbole, like in the TV shows.

"That's more than a coincidence for this small town. The only commodity here is water, or maybe a beach," Ramsey replied.

"That's what we thought."

"Do you have the time of the calls?" Ramsey wanted to put a perspective on the new people in Parker Moore's life and the events in his house.

"Let's see." The supervisor paused. "There was one Saturday night. One Sunday morning ..."

Ramsey stopped him. "Wait, Sunday morning? What time?"

"Um, it was ..." A long pause ensued.

Ramsey pulled out a pen and paper. No notes was the rule, but he'd trash it after.

"Yeah, here it is. 8:30 a.m. Does that help?" The supervisor was now curious.

"Yes. There is someone else. Can you pinpoint an address?" Ramsey wouldn't need to write that down.

"I'll get on it. Ramsey? One more thing. We got John. You'll see him when you get back here. Take care of yourself." John Mansfield hung up.

Ramsey sat in silence for a moment. His usual hard shell softened and his eyes teared when he heard the good news about his partner. He never heard about the third call.

It was 3:00 p.m.

22

"Okay, Moore. You've got one more chance with me. A senator's chief of staff was poisoned. We have a man identified as Pierre Simon from Corsica, posing as said chief of staff in Petoskey, looking like he was trying to kill you. We have another man, John Sanchez from Arizona, in the ICU, unconscious, who did try to kill you. And somebody in town, who we don't know about, trying to protect you—and so far the only person congruent to all of this is you. Why? We're the FBI and we have no clue yet." Fletcher was back in the Public Safety office interview room with his suit jacket off, his old-fashioned shoulder holster flapping as he paced back and forth in front of Parker. Tim Johnson sat at the table across from Parker.

"Agent Fletcher, you have my file. You've had a file on me since I was with the police department in Ann Arbor. You know all about my past. I do not know why I'm involved in any of this." Parker sat quietly to purposely piss off Fletcher.

"Are you trying to piss me off, Moore? Cause you're doing a really good job of it." Fletcher was staring at Parker as he leaned on the table with both palms. His face was inches from Parker's left eye.

Silence.

"They both worked for a security firm out of Texas." Fletcher stood up and was walking away from Parker and Johnson as he talked. "We're looking into their contracts now."

"I haven't been to Texas since I was eighteen years old," Parker retorted. He was staring into Tim Johnson's eyes.

"They're ex-military, for Christ's sake. Doesn't that concern you in the least, Mr. Moore?" Fletcher's manner was quieter but he was not less frustrated.

Silence.

In a quieter tone, Fletcher noted, "I would advise you to watch what you eat and drink around people you don't know." He was standing against the wall behind Parker with his arms folded. "Mark Fairchild was poisoned with sarin. You're an intelligent man, Moore. I don't think I have to explain that to you. I'm going back to D.C. for a couple of days."

Parker was amazed that Fletcher really didn't know about his NSA days. Ramsey and Brooks had told Parker that his work around the country was completely out of the normal channels of United States intelligence for very specific reasons. Parker now wished somebody would tell him what was really going on.

It was now after 6:00 p.m. Fletcher put on his jacket and was ready to leave the room.

"Jack, I will—"

"Will what?" Fletcher cut off Tim Johnson. "You're as useless as two tits on a bull. I'll be back Saturday. If our man wakes up at the hospital, call me." Fletcher was walking through the door when a uniformed Petoskey police officer walked in.

"Chief. Guy at the hospital just died."

"Still want me to call you, Jack?" Johnson said to Fletcher who stopped in the doorway to listen.

"Kiss my ass," Fletcher yelled as he walked down the hall.

Johnson looked at Parker. "Well, now. I think that went well. Asshole," Johnson said as he nodded his head back toward the door Fletcher just exited through. "Parker, what am I going to do with you?"

Parker Moore was still sitting in the chair at the table. His hands were in his lap and he was looking directly at Johnson. He got up and said, "Let me go home. I need some time."

Tim Johnson grabbed Parker by the arm as he went by. "When's Sam coming home?"

"Saturday."

"Let's hope this is over before that." He let go of Parker's arm.

Johnson remained seated as Parker started out the door and down the hallway. He turned and yelled out the door, "Stuart's with you tonight!"

Parker waved his hand up in the air to acknowledge Johnson as he continued to walk down the hall.

23

Parker walked up Lake Street, across US-31, up Howard, and finally up Mitchell, and home. He looked at the ground almost the entire way. Everything in Petoskey was uphill from the harbor area. His shadows drove by slowly, turned around, and parked facing west on Mitchell Street in front of his house. They watched as Parker went inside.

Pete Stuart was waiting for him. Parker grabbed his gym bag and walked back toward the front door. It was time to work off some stress.

The drive up Mitchell Street was quick for Ramsey. He'd been watching the clinics for people coming and going while Parker was being interviewed by Fletcher. He also checked the houses on Mitchell Street that had a view of Parker's house. One was a boardinghouse and two others had for-sale signs out front. Nothing looked suspicious at first glance. After he drove past Parker's house and saw the Malibu out front, he decided to head back to the Perry for some dinner. But first, he parked in front of City Hall and walked into the Public Safety office.

"Hello. Todd Ramsey. I'd like to speak with Tim Johnson, if he's available." Todd Ramsey was dressed in a blue suit.

The clerk was already on overtime and was trying to leave, but she put on her best smile. Her coat was already on.

"Sure. Sure. Let me see—we actually were supposed to be closed for the night, but I'll check."

She picked up the phone and dialed Johnson's extension.

Johnson picked up. "Yes?"

"There's a Mister Todd Ramsey here to see you."

"About what? I'm tired."

She turned toward Ramsey. "He's wondering what you're here for."

"Tell him I'm here about Parker Moore." Ramsey stood quietly with his hands at his side.

"Director, it's about Parker Moore."

Before the name Moore was finished coming out of her mouth, Tim Johnson had rounded the corner to the front reception area. He looked at Ramsey and immediately knew this was important.

"Mr. Ramsey, I'm Director Johnson. Why don't you come back here into the conference room?"

The two men shook hands and walked down the hallway. The receptionist pointed to her watch and Tim Johnson waved at her to leave. The Petoskey Public Safety offices were closed at night. All dispatch was handled out of the county 911 system. It was just Johnson and Ramsey alone in the building at 7:13 p.m.

She sat at her dining room table. She'd just finished soldering the last wires into the circuit. Her cell phone was turned off. She had been apprised that the calls might be traced.

It was 3:30 a.m. in Dubai. Sir Edward Framingham couldn't sleep. He paced back and forth in front of his bedroom window. He wore a long navy robe over his black silk pajamas. The Hendrick's gin in his left hand was working to take his anxiety away. In his right hand was the cell phone. He'd been trying all night to reach his contact. The calls had been going directly to voicemail.

24

Parker Moore needed a regular night. Since Saturday his routine had been off. He was back to scrambling and waking up worried about the day instead of enjoying every moment. Sam was gone, which added to the worry; but she was out of harm's way. Her presence added a steadiness and security Parker had come to depend on. He walked out the front door to go to the gym with Stuart in tow. The Malibu stayed put until the two were halfway downtown.

The rope and tackle on the flagpole at the library banged against the metal in the evening breeze. As Parker and Stuart walked toward the gym, Parker changed his mind.

"Hey, Mark, can I set this stuff here for a little bit until I get back?" Parker set his gym bag in the cubby by the front door of Center City Gym.

"No problem, buddy. Whatever you want, Parker. The place is yours." Mark was entertaining some regular members by the tables in front of the window. He waved to Parker and smiled.

"I need some water time, Stuart."

"No problem. You lead the way." Stuart wasn't dressed for the colder breeze by the harbor, but he didn't have much of a choice if that's where Parker was headed. He waved to his fellow officers in the Malibu and pointed to the harbor. They turned right on Petoskey Street and headed toward the boat launch parking.

"Pete, how much do you know?"

"About what?" Stuart was looking around as he and Parker walked through Pennsylvania Park. It was dark, and since it was a Wednesday the park was empty.

"You know. Me. The reason you're with me."

"Honestly? Not much. We were put on this detail as bodyguards because the only other thing to do is lock you up, which we do know you refused. Other than that, nothing."

"Are you scared?"

"Let's say this detail is not uncommon to the three of us since we do it for the governor, but this does feel different. Nobody in recent memory has tried to kill the governor. You're at four times in four years." Pete Stuart was six feet tall and weighed two hundred and twenty pounds of pure muscle. If he was afraid, he didn't show it.

"I'm mad. In fact, I'm pissed off. I feel like I'm being set up on purpose." Parker looked toward American Spoon through the park as they passed the gazebo and turned left on Lake Street.

The stiff wind off the bay hit them just as they cleared the park. The wind traveled up Lake Street west to east. Stuart zipped up his jacket and fixed his collar around his neck. Parker's Alaskan blood had him with his coat open and not even flinching as they walked into the wind.

"Sorry to put you through this. I just need some peace. We're going to the end of the pier, if you need to know that."

"We're good. Boys are down there already." Stuart felt confident and comfortable.

Laura finished her work in the house and walked out the front door. As she sauntered down the steps, she noticed there were no cars in front of Parker's house. As she walked west down Mitchell Street, there was nobody else outside. Only lights on in front rooms and bedrooms in the neighborhood.

Parker and Stuart made their way out to the bench at the end of the pier. The Malibu was parked in the dark at the rear of the boat launch against the retaining wall. The lights of the harbor sparkled as they reflected off the black water. The waves lapped against the cement break wall. Behind them, the subtle sounds of the town up the hill. Light traffic headed north and south on US-31. The traffic lights cycled red to green with no cars at the intersection most of the time.

The stars were out. A new moon left the sky dark above the lights. To the north, Harbor Springs glistened. Nubs Nob and Boyne Highlands were dormant, awaiting snow.

"Pete, I've been through everything imaginable short of war. I've pulled guns on people. I've wrestled people trying to hurt me. Tackled criminals on the street. Found suicides. Run companies. Lobbied. Coached. Had my youngest kid thirty feet from a grizzly walking at him with its head shaking like he was gonna eat him, and I stepped in between. Got in trouble. Faced everything. Now? I feel like I don't know shit. Two people in three days have died at my house, and I don't know why."

Parker stared into the black water. He sat slumped over with his forearms and hands between his knees. Stuart was sitting straight up and never stopped looking around. Pete Stuart did not respond. It wasn't his way. He just looked at Parker and waited for more. Nothing came. The two sat in silence for the next twenty minutes.

Todd Ramsey was leaving Tim Johnson's office. It was 9:15 p.m. "Are we square?" Ramsey said to Johnson as he stood in the doorway.

"Yes we are, Agent Ramsey. As Parker Moore might say quoting from *Casablanca*, 'this time I think our side will win'." He smiled and shook Ramsey's hand.

Ramsey got into his car and drove to Mitchell Street. He was more confident about keeping Parker alive now that everyone was on the same page. And he wasn't worried about Tim Johnson being connected to the assassins.

He passed Parker and Stuart walking into the gym, so he headed to Parker's house. He wasn't going to allow for a repeat of someone getting inside and ruining another night.

"Morgue, Clawson." Was the answer at the hospital?

"Clawson, Johnson. Anyone claim him yet?" Tim Johnson was making one last call before he left the office.

"No, sir. Not even a phone call. He's still here."

"Thanks. Oh, and if anyone …"

"Got it, Director. I'll let you know."

"See ya." Johnson ended the conversation.

"Is that enough?" the man asked Clawson after he hung up the phone.

"Maybe another thousand." Clawson was holding a wad of bills.

"You're buying a big hit here," said the stranger.

"Yeah, but I really need the cash." Clawson collected the rest of the money and put it in a nondescript file in the back of one of the many drawers in the morgue. He didn't want anyone to find the money in his pocket while he was knocked out.

"You ready?" The stranger had on dark blue clothing, a navy blue baseball cap, and black driving gloves.

"Ready— Wait. You knock me out, take the body, and I get the money. Okay, now." Clawson was standing steady with his eyes closed.

In a flash the blackjack struck Clawson just at the right angle to knock him out and send him crumpled to the floor. Clawson never saw the .22 Walther that was used to finish the job. The man reached his gloved hand into the drawer and took his money back.

25

She walked up the sidewalk and stairs to Parker's front door. A few lights were on inside; so she knocked.

"Can I help you, miss?" said a man getting out of a black Buick.

"No. I'm here to visit Parker. Can I help *you*?" Laura returned the question.

"No. I'm here to see him, too. Let's see if he's home." Todd Ramsey knocked on the door.

Laura was somewhat indignant. She had plans, and they did not include this guy.

"Guess he's not home after all. I'm sorry for being rude. I'm David Jones. I'm writing a book on the Great Lakes and was going to speak with Parker."

"Laura. I work with Parker."

"Well, no sense making it a lost cause. I haven't had dinner yet. Do you want to get a drink?" Todd Ramsey was by no means plain or ugly, and he had used his looks in the field before for close reconnaissance.

"With you?" Laura was taken off guard. She quickly glanced at the door as if wishing someone would answer it; then she turned back toward Ramsey and shrugged her shoulders. "Sure, why not."

Ramsey held his right arm out to direct Laura down the stairs and onto the sidewalk. He followed close behind, examining every inch of the woman before him. His left hand was tightly holding a .22 in his coat pocket.

As the alarm went off next to the bed, Jim Reegan was already awake and looking at the ceiling. He hadn't slept all night. He picked up the phone next to him. It was 7:00 a.m. in Dubai.

"Edward? Meet me for coffee in our suite. I'll be there in five minutes."

Sir Edward was still in his pajamas and robe. He was on his third Hendricks on ice.

Both men made their respective way to the meeting suite they'd purchased five years ago, knowing the United States Supreme Court would change the method political action committee money could be accounted for. They had just moved into the building this past August, as soon as the building was completed.

"I haven't been able to reach our contact. What is going on?" Sir Edward was physically calm but verbally frustrated.

"We've been told that our people have been shadowed and they believe phones have been listened to," was Reegan's reply as he poured an orange juice. He took the bottle and showed it to Framingham, offering some.

"No. No, thank you. I'm not done drinking."

"Our contact in D.C. believes it's the FBI, but I'm not so sure. So far, we've been lucky. But when Fairchild threatened to go public, when we decided not to give him more money, that put more focus on the senator he was working for and the investigation he was on. Suddenly, the other two deaths connected to the same investigation become pertinent and bingo, the Feds are on it."

"But that is FBI territory. Why would you believe otherwise?" Sir Edward poured another Hendricks, although he added some orange juice this time. Reegan was lying on the leather sofa, resting with his left arm behind his head. His right hand swirled the orange juice in his glass on an oval-shaped coffee table.

"Breakfast?" Reegan smiled when he saw the orange juice added to the gin.

"I'll take my nourishment wherever I can. Now, you were saying?"

"Well, the way I see it, one of the other intelligence groups is in on this. If it was the FBI, they'd just go around and arrest everybody and anybody they could. One of the other groups isn't above using human decoys. The FBI has already been checking our security company. It's just a matter of days before they bring in the moving van and take all the files. They won't find anything, of course."

The group had just purchased the Blackwater Security Company, made infamous for some security disasters in Iraq. Now the group not only controlled the political action committee money in order to get to the only vulnerable spot of the American people—their government—it also controlled the security giant to protect its interests in the Middle East and around the world once the American forces went home.

"If we allow him to live, will we survive what might come out at the next committee meeting?"

"Money buys a lot, but I'm afraid the mood of the American public right now wouldn't stand for a group of ten people in Dubai shaping their government. We have two branches and need the third." Reegan was looking at Framingham sitting in a leather chair across from the sofa.

"We own the media. We own several on the Senate floor and in the House; and the American public rarely shows up to vote—so why should we worry?"

"Because, Sir Edward, when their feet are held to the fire, Americans will band together. It will become a media circus, one group investigating another group, and through it all our influence stops. We have invested billions. We have silenced people. And we are only one year away from owning the White House. Our investors around the world would not be happy if we pulled the plug now." Reegan sat up.

"Right, then. I just hope the contacts and the contracts hold up their end of the bargain." Sir Edward tipped his glass all the way back and downed the last of the Hendricks and orange juice. "What happened in Yemen, by the way?" Sir Edward couldn't get that one out of his craw.

"Just some leftover people and staff we didn't weed out very well in our takeover of the company. Our ruse was working as we suspected. We received no response from the State Department or anyone else, so we thought we would just quietly eliminate a probable CIA agent in the name of a new radical group. We're pretty sure they got him back, though. We think he was only around a short while before we got word from the employment group in Dubai that he was new and unchecked. It pays to offer people a lot of money to tell us things." Reegan seemed undisturbed by the whole thing.

"And if he shows up somewhere down the road?" Sir Edward wasn't comfortable yet.

"So? We own half the world right now and we can buy the other half. No one can put us anywhere with any connection." Reegan was still calm and confident.

"Almost no one." Sir Edward said, staring at Reegan.

"Time for a real breakfast?" Reegan was standing in his white robe and stretching.

"Sleep. Time for sleep. I'll see you this evening. Good day, Mr. Reegan." Sir Edward exited the room by way of the private elevator.

Jim Reegan grabbed his new encrypted phone from his pocket. The message was concise:

Bodies gone. Next in play.

He put the phone back in his robe pocket and picked up the house phone on the coffee table.

"Henri? Can you bring me my usual for breakfast? Thanks."

He was waking up as he felt the landing gear hit the runway. The plane carrying John Brooks was landing at Langley Air Force Base in Virginia late at night. A car was waiting for him. The trip to Ft. Meade, Maryland, would be another three hours; so there was plenty of time to wake and prepare for the next day's debriefing.

Senator Henry paced in his Foggy Bottom apartment across from George Washington University Hospital. He was a graduate of GW Law and held a fond remembrance of his days there. He had vowed to come back in an influential role—and had. Now, he couldn't stop thinking about how influential that role had become. The NSA had some loose leads to the people who killed his old colleague Stimson, and some unverified information about a leak within the Super PAC. Two people could put all of it out in public view, and they were both two days away.

He heard a buzz and grabbed the cell from his pocket. It wasn't that phone. On the dresser in his bedroom was the other phone.

Landed. 8:00 am tomorrow.

"Okay now. One in, one still to get," he quietly said to himself as he sat down in the chair by the large bay window. The streets were quiet. David Henry, the high school football hero from Warner Robins, Georgia, took a long deep breath and watched the lights twinkle in the night sky over Washington, D.C.

26

"How's the beer?" Todd Ramsey asked his new acquaintance.

"Good. Good," said Laura as she put the pint of Guinness down. She was sitting with her legs crossed under the bar. She wore blue jeans and a dark green cowl-neck sweater.

"What is it you do, where Parker consults?"

"I'm the biller and coder for the physicians. Not a lot of excitement, but it pays the bills." She was extraordinarily confident for someone with a complete stranger.

The only place still cooking dinner late on a Wednesday night that Todd Ramsey liked was the Noggin Room at the Perry Hotel. They also knew him as Mr. Jones, so it would be easy to keep his cover.

"You?" Again Laura returned the question.

"My book? It's no secret the Great Lakes are big business, and I'd like to make sure we protect them. That simple, really."

"Married?"

"No. You?" Ramsey said looking into Laura's dark eyes.

"No." She sipped her beer and looked at the menu.

"So, what can I get you folks?"

"Burger for me. Medium. Chips; no fries. I'm going to the rest room, so whatever the lady wants." Ramsey stood up and walked behind the bar toward the rest room. He stood for a few moments to watch his new friend through the lattice that acted as the back wall of the bar before you stepped down into the dining room.

"I guess I'll have the same. Thanks." Laura looked up at the TV. She checked her cell phone for messages, then looked back at the TV.

Ramsey, satisfied, headed to the rest room.

"How about a nightcap?" Parker and Pete Stuart were back from the gym and sitting in the media room watching the Red Wings

"Where?"

"City Park. Let's go visit ole' Ernest over the bar."

"Let me get with the others." Stuart walked into the dark living room with his cell phone at his ear. He looked outside toward the curb in front of the house where the white van was parked.

"Well?" Parker asked.

"We're good. They'll head over and be set up."

"Let's go." The two men grabbed their coats and walked out the door.

"Here's your burgers. Anything else I can get for you right now?" asked the bartender.

"I think we're good. Thanks." Todd Ramsey was back from the rest room.

"How long you in town?" Laura wondered

"Not sure. A week. Maybe a month. Could be a year." Ramsey was just about to take his first bite.

"Vague. I see." Laura was picking at her chips.

"You?"

"I'm here for good now. Got a decent thing going with the temp agency, and I like the area."

Ramsey was fully into the burger now and looked up to glance at the hockey game on the TV. The Red Wings were still playing on the west coast.

"I'll take another." Laura held her empty pint glass up to the bartender.

"Men?" Ramsey asked.

"Excuse me?" Laura quickly turned to Ramsey and glared at him.

"Men. Any men in your life?" Ramsey was still looking at the TV screen.

"No. Women?"

"No." Ramsey turned back to Laura. She was smiling at him.

Laura took a big bite into the burger as she looked straight ahead. The lettuce and tomato started to squirt out of the bun. She had to stop biting and catch the innards of the sandwich before they plopped on her plate.

"Whoa! That's attractive." Ramsey was watching the game but caught the food folly out of the corner of his eye.

"I'm so glad I said yes to you," Laura said facetiously as she rearranged her burger on the plate. She was circling the sandwich with her eyes to make sure all was in place prior to the next bite. "I did meet a guy a while back. He just up and left the other day. Poof. Gone. Like he was never here."

"You wanna get outta here?" Ramsey was finished and drank the last of his Founder's Red Eye.

"Can I finish?" Laura was perturbed but excited.

"Sure. I'm gonna make a call. Be right back."

Parker and Stuart sat at the front corner of the bar at City Park Grill. Jason walked over to shake Parker's hand.

"Parker."

"Jason. This is Pete Stuart."

"My pleasure. Everything good tonight?" Jason was making sure they had their drinks.

"Yes, thanks." Parker took a sip of his Glenfidich. He was trying to be nonchalant with Stuart at his side; so there was the usual banter with Jason.

Pete Stuart was nursing a club soda. "I'm good."

"Jason, you got a minute?" Parker slid away from the bar. He looked at Stuart. "Okay?" he asked.

"Sure. I'll be right here. Damn." He was watching the TV in the left corner of the ceiling. The Sharks just tied the game.

Parker and Jason headed for the back office. The other two shadows were busy talking with two female acquaintances at a table toward the back of the room. Parker winked at them as he went through the green curtain toward the manager's office.

"Jason," Parker whispered when they were in his office. "Is that tunnel that runs out toward the Perry Hotel still open?"

"Sorry, Parker. All bricked up." Jason looked around, smiled, and moved closer to Parker. "But, the rear emergency entrance alarm is off," he whispered.

"I owe you, Jason," Parker said softly as he swiftly walked out the door.

27

"Director, there was one more thing I wanted to add." Ramsey was standing outside the side door of the Noggin Room on the sidewalk looking south toward Pennsylvania Park.

"Ramsey. Before you start, I've got a situation. Both bodies are gone. Our perps have vanished." Tim Johnson was at the hospital standing outside the morgue.

Ramsey was silent. It was close to midnight and Johnson was tired.

"Ramsey, you there?" Johnson was not happy. His voice was loud and stern. "The guy here was shot. We're checking the security cameras now. The guy in Gaylord just vanished." Johnson was upset, to the point he kept repeating himself.

"I got it," said Ramsey as he scanned the area. "Johnson? Johnson? Tim!?" Ramsey couldn't get the normally calm Director of Public Safety to stop talking.

"What?" Johnson finally yelled back. His shirt and tie were rumpled and his trench coat hung open with the belt dragging on the floor.

"I got it. Tomorrow's the day. I've eliminated one more suspect. At least, I think I have. Are we straight for tomorrow?" Ramsey was anxious to return to his date.

"Yes. Yes, we are. Sorry. I'm a little pissed right now. How the fuck do you lose two bodies? How!?"

Parker ran down the back alley. There were no side windows facing Pennsylvania Park, so he casually walked around the parking lot to the west until he reached Lake Street, where he stopped and looked both ways, like a child running away from school to play hooky. He walked north through the park; then he started to jog. He wasn't sure why he was heading in that direction.

"What the hell?" The closer he got to the Perry Hotel, he recognized Ramsey. He stopped dead in his tracks.

"Parker? What are you doing out here at this hour?"

Parker turned to see who was behind him. "Catherine!? I— I was just going to meet a friend." He looked back toward the Perry. Ramsey was gone.

"Hey, are you okay?" Catherine was standing close. Both of her hands were in the pockets of her long wool coat.

"Yes. I just thought I saw a friend."

"Friend? Seems like I've seen you with someone at your side ever since our meeting the other day." Catherine was looking around as she spoke.

"I'm popular. What can I say?" Parker watched Catherine closely.

"So, heading my way?" Catherine smiled as she grabbed Parker's arm and brought him close. Her right hand stayed in her pocket.

"Sure. Sure." They started to walk east on Bay Street. Parker took one more look behind him. Nothing.

Stuart looked around and saw his two fellow officers sitting in the rear of the Grill. He saw Jason walk by their table.

"Where's Moore?" Pete Stuart quickly jumped down from his stool.

"Ah, I don't know," Jason replied.

"Shit. You guys go east. I'll head toward the water." The three men ran out of the bar.

Jason just shook his head and started putting chairs on top of tables. It was closing time.

"So, Parker, aren't you married?" Catherine had her left arm tucked between Parker's right bicep and his chest.

"Yes."

"And, she is where?"

"Idaho. Visiting her daughter." Parker realized his phone was still at home and he hadn't talked with Sam all day.

They were walking south on Division toward the Crooked Tree Art Center and the library.

"I live right up on Mitchell. How about a drink?" Catherine's voice was soft in the cool fall air. The wind that buffeted Parker and Stuart when they sat at the waterfront was gone. It was quiet. Still. There was no traffic to be seen or heard. Catherine snuggled closer to Parker.

"What?" Parker was suddenly preoccupied. Who was this woman and why had he escaped his protectors? He felt he needed to find his real shadow; he was convinced that was Ramsey.

"A drink. Just friends. Nothing more. We're going in the same direction." Catherine turned them east on Mitchell in front of the Presbyterian Church.

Stuart stood at the edge of the waterfront park and looked toward the end of the pier, squinting to see if anyone was out there. After checking the downtown area, the two officers in the white van slowly drove up Bay Street looking in between and at each house. They just missed Parker and Catherine walk across the street in front of the church.

"Catherine, I'll walk you home, but I'll wait on the drink until Sam gets home. We'd love to join you then." Parker was calculating. It was Ramsey; somehow he had to get back to the Perry to find him, without raising the suspicion of this woman. This woman?

"Parker? Parker Moore?" Todd Ramsey walked out from the side alley of the church.

"Hey." Parker didn't use a name in return.

"Jones. David Jones. I'm writing the book on the Great Lakes. We've been trading phone calls."

"Sure. David." Parker stuck out his right hand and grabbed Ramsey's to shake. "I'm glad to see you."

"Parker." Catherine tugged at Parker's coat.

"Oh, this is Catherine … Catherine, I don't remember your last name."

"Hamilton. Catherine Hamilton. Have we met?" she smiled at Ramsey but wondered why someone would be out this late in a town that usually closed its doors by ten during the week. And why was he coming out of an alley?

"Ms. Hamilton." Ramsey knew where she lived and that she often went out at night; so he kept his attention on Parker. "Sorry, Mr. Moore. I've been staying at the apartment next to the church here and was just coming home when I saw you."

"Jones! Hey, Jones!" Laura was walking up Mitchell Street in front of the Crooked Tree Arts Center when she spotted Ramsey.

The three people turned and watched her run across the street.

"You stiffed me for the bill! What the hell are you doing here, Moore? Aren't you that woman …"

"Yes. Catherine Hamilton," she interrupted. "We met at the clinic a few mornings ago. Well, this is suddenly a crowded street. I'll just continue on home. Nice meeting you—Mr. Jones, was it?"

"Yes." Ramsey nodded at her.

"See you, Catherine." Parker waved as she walked away.

"So, Jones, is that your idea of a first date? Asshole. Catherine, wait up! I'm going your way." Laura jogged in her tight jeans and heels and caught up with Catherine.

"What the fuck is going on?" Parker was a step ahead of Todd Ramsey.

"That's a nice hello for someone who's been keeping you alive." Ramsey looked around and grabbed Parker by the arm. He dragged him across the street. They were only two houses from home when the white van raced up and parked on the wrong side of the street in front of Parker's house. Two men jumped out, drew their guns, and charged at Ramsey and Parker.

"Down! Now!" The Glocks in the officers' hands were visible and Ramsey and Parker lay flat on their abdomens.

"Moore! What the hell are you doing?" Stuart came running from behind.

"Hold it, boys. I'm going to get up." Parker stood. "Todd. Get up."

Tim Johnson drove up and got out. Ramsey was being stood up by Stuart. The two other officers still had their weapons at center mass level with Ramsey.

"Okay. Okay. Let's get off the street. Holster your weapons. Up to Moore's, now! Everybody," ordered Johnson.

Johnson got back in his car and drove up the alley behind Parker's house and pulled into the drive. One of the officers repositioned the white van so that it faced the right direction, and everyone made their way into the house.

Catherine and Laura had stopped at Summit to watch the show.

28

Pete Stuart settled into the dining room chair alongside his two colleagues. Parker sat alone on the other side of the table. Todd Ramsey leaned against the arched entry from the front of the house. Tim Johnson took off his trench coat and pulled up a chair to the table. He turned it backwards and sat down, grasping the high back in front of him with both hands.

"Gentlemen, meet Todd Ramsey, National Security Agency. He's the shooter of our first victim, and the shadow we've wondered about." Johnson looked haggard. He'd been up for over twenty-four hours now.

Parker checked his cell phone. He only half listened to Johnson. Three missed calls and four messages. The last text:

Worried about you. Where are you?

"Can you guys give me a couple minutes? I need to check on the cats, and text Sam." Parker got up from the table and walked into the kitchen. He opened a can of Friskies. As soon as he popped the top off, Kali and Keeper came running down the stairs, past the strange men, and into the kitchen. Parker divided the cat food onto two dishes and put them on the floor. As the cats ate, he texted Sam:

Good. Late gym night and drinks at City Park with friends. Night honey.

He didn't know what to say so he kept it short. He looked at the cats, took a deep breath, and returned to the dining room.

"Ramsey filled the boys in on what's been going on. We'll all be around you tomorrow, Parker, but not with you. You doing okay?" Johnson yawned. It was now after 1:00 a.m.

"Just tired."

"Stuart's staying tonight. What's a normal Thursday for you?" Johnson talked while the others listened. Todd Ramsey had found a seat at the table.

"I volunteer at St. Francis at 9:00 a.m.; then I usually come back and eat some breakfast before I head out to Conway, Harbor, and then back to Petoskey. Why?"

"We're going to have people at each site before you get there. Parker, I think you've been used as bait, but I can't fix that." Ramsey was trying to interject what he thought, but not what he knew.

"Geez, it didn't take a genius to figure that out," Parker sniped back. He looked at his phone to make sure he caught everything. "Wait, there's a message from Steve Brown about my new tires being ready. I gotta get my tires."

"Fine," Ramsey said. "That's actually good. I'm convinced whatever's going to happen will be at one of your normal stops. Make sure you get your tires early. That'll show everyone you're just out doing a normal thing on a normal day."

"Do we actually know who the person is?" Pete Stuart asked Tim Johnson.

"Agent?" Johnson looked at Ramsey.

"I believe I do." Todd Ramsey shared nothing more.

29

She walked around the house to make sure all was in order. The house would look as if no one had ever been inside. The rent was paid under a fictitious name and bags were packed and already in the car. She looked at the clock. 1:55 a.m. In about twelve hours, she'd be wealthy and headed for the Caymans.

Todd Ramsey drove down Mitchell Street for a final look. The entire neighborhood was dark except for one house.

Tim Johnson was finally home. He dropped his trench coat on a chair, threw his clothes into the laundry, and got into the shower. The hot water began to relax him. He put both hands on the wall in front of him and let the water run over his head. He was trying not to run all the scenarios through his head.

The white van sat in front of Parker's house and a brown van kept watch in the alley. Pete Stuart dozed off in the living room. He was startled awake when Keeper came up to his hand hanging down on the loveseat and rubbed his head against it.

"Took a while, eh buddy? Don't worry. Everything's gonna be fine." Stuart petted Keeper's head while the cat sat down and began to purr.

Parker lay in bed and stared at the ceiling. He thought of everything the NSA had listened to during the year Parker had worn the wire. He remembered the death threats from people he dealt with. He ran through every meeting and every conversation and situation he'd been a part of. The Stimson meeting. The conversation he had before Stimson's demise. The secretary carrying a clipboard and writing down everything Parker did. The governor of Alaska's bodyguard staring at him and making notes. The Silverbow Inn.

"What the ..." Parker sat up in bed. "The Silverbow."

He recalled hearing a conversation between two men who didn't know Parker was in the backroom of the restaurant with them. One of the men had a strong British accent. They discussed oil, leases, money, and the manipulation of all three. Soon after, the Alaskan governor had a new bodyguard and the office staff changed before she left office. Somebody knew Parker had been there. His secret didn't die with Stimson. Whoever it was, wanted Parker dead.

He reached over and grabbed the phone. It was midnight in Idaho. He texted Sam:

I love you more than anything.

Then he lay down and fell asleep.

30

THURSDAY ~ OCTOBER 27

"What? What?" Parker was sprawled face down on the queen-sized Tempur-Pedic. It was the only time of day his large frame would be comfortable. He was sunk into the mattress and didn't want to move. Kali stood on his back.

He opened one eye and looked at the clock. 7:06 a.m. He turned on the radio. News about the governor of Illinois awaiting his sentencing. Parker grimaced as he remembered those days and nights; the horrible events that went with them. Michigan was done and put to bed. Illinois was just finishing with its governor. Alaska? Why the hell was all of this happening again?

"Bullshit." He threw off the covers and Kali leapt for the door. She turned around to look at him. Parker got up, turned on the light on, and headed for the shower. "Pete? I'm up."

"Okay. Coffee's on." Pete Stuart was already in the kitchen opening up a can of cat food. "There's more than one way to skin a cat. No pun intended, guys." He looked down at his new friend, Keeper. Kali kept her distance and stood partially hidden by the door-wall curtains.

"I think I know what's going on. *And* I think I know why someone's after me. It's all about oil!" Parker walked down the stairs calm and confident. He reached into the cupboard for a cereal bowl and his coffee mug. He stopped and looked at Stuart. "The only problem is, I don't know who they are. I mean, I think I know who some of them are—but together? That's the mystery." He reached above the microwave into the cupboard for his Grape-Nuts cereal.

"Whoever they are, they're very serious." Pete sat on the kitchen stool holding his coffee mug. "Why oil?"

"It's a long story. Too long." Parker reached into his pocket for his phone.

Morning Doll!

He texted Sam back and called Steve Brown. Today was about doing normal activities.

"Parker! What the hell you doing up so early?" Steve had just walked into his office. The service department at Brown Motors was already open.

"Hey, can I come in right after my church thing to get those tires?" Parker crunched his cereal in between words.

"Sure. No problem. Sam still in Idaho?"

"Yup." A gulp of coffee.

"Ten fifteen work?" Steve heard the crunching. "What are you chewing, ice?"

"Grape-Nuts. See you then." Parker closed his phone.

"Moore, the director wanted you to have this." Stuart pulled a .38 Chief's Special out of his bag and held it out to Parker.

"No. If it comes down to that, I'm already dead." Parker went to the sink and rinsed his bowl. He looked out the window into the sunlight just starting to come up over the neighborhood. "Besides, it's gonna be all right." He turned to Stuart. "It'll be all right." Parker smiled and started for his coat.

"All right, but when you walk out that door, I'm not with you." Stuart looked at the nickel-plated Smith and Wesson in his hand.

"No. But everybody in a lot of cars will be." Parker smiled as he walked through the sliding glass door onto the deck. He closed it behind him and waved at Pete. Once he cleared the garage and walked into the alley, he stopped and looked around. The morning air was brisk and the sky was a bright blue with a smattering of grayish purple clouds floating around. The kind of fall day that watercolor artists like to paint. He saw the brown van at the bottom of the alley on Woodland. "Okay. Here we go."

It was 8:55 a.m.

31

John Brooks walked into the NSA building. Before he reached the screening area, he was met by his supervisor, John Mansfield, and a host of others who welcomed him back. After processing his credentials and heading to a conference room, Brooks sat for a moment and took in his surroundings. He was a field agent. As good on the computer as anyone else connected to NSA, he was never comfortable in the same place for long, and especially not confined in a conference room or cubicle. But today was different. He could spend the whole day here and like it. What he did not know was that he was twenty-four hours from being eliminated back in Yemen.

"Good to see you, John," Mansfield said as he placed two cups of coffee on the table.

"Thanks." Brooks took a sip of coffee. "Ah, office swill. I missed it so." Brooks said with a wide grin.

"So, what did ya tell State?"

"I told them that the FBI should be looking for a Yemen-connected cartel wishing to establish a revolutionary front inside the U.S. while trying to gain the good graces of people in Syria, Iran, and Al-Qaeda. That's why I was in Yemen trying to intercept communications while looking for the American side of the group." Brooks had his chair leaned back on two legs while he held the coffee cup with two hands. His blue shirt and pants were wrinkled. He also wore the Air Force baseball cap the tactical group that brought him back stateside had given him.

Mansfield sat hunched over with his hands and forearms resting on the table as he intently listened to Brooks. Once he heard his answer, he sat back and laughed. "So, bullshit?"

"More or less. If the FBI was in on this, the whole world would know about the PAC. I know that. We all know that; so they're still chasing."

Mansfield sat forward with most of his upper body leaning over the table toward John Brooks. His cardigan sweater was unbuttoned and his polo shirt was fully opened at the collar. "Now ... what do we know?"

Brooks sat forward and put his coffee down. "North Channel Oil and Gulf Coast Petroleum have put together this group. It's their version of a Super PAC—only they've been funneling money for five years—well before the Supreme Court made its infamous decision. The head of this OPEC-based group is Sir Edward Framingham of North Channel. Their security is headed up by Jim Reegan of Gulf Coast. In fact, the guys who grabbed me tried to look like they were from Yemen, but body types, hair, mannerisms—lots of things—indicated they weren't." Brooks was almost excited to finally tell what he knew. His usual calm abandoned him for the moment.

"Your information is right on, John. Todd's with your boy Moore in Michigan. People coming after him like he has the plague. Both guys, now dead, were ex-military and former spooks; one lived in the Southwest somewhere and the other was from Corsica. FBI's been running down those leads. We already made a connection with phone calls between a security company connected to Gulf Coast Oil. The calls emanated from Michigan; actually from Moore's street, where we're holding him out as bait." Mansfield's voice was quiet and controlled. At the end, his face became a little twisted. "What exactly does he know?"

John Brooks stood up to stretch. He walked the length of the conference table with his hands behind his head. He came around the table and stood behind Mansfield. He leaned down and whispered into Mansfield's left ear. "He's the only one who can put Sir Edward and Reegan together in Juneau before the governor resigned and everyone got rich."

"They did kill Stimson?" asked Mansfield.

"Yes. Stimson was about to push for drilling in the 1002 Area of ANWR and had the votes." Brooks moved back around the table and sat down. His calm demeanor had returned.

"But that area is projected to barely change the economic impact on the price of crude." Mansfield was familiar with the Arctic National Wildlife Refuge in Alaska. When he was in the Air Force, based at Eielson in Fairbanks, he flew over it often.

"Maybe to you and me, but when you control most of the world's pricing and distribution, it turns into billions of dollars lost at the gas pumps," explained Brooks. "Let's face it, John, when there's a burp in the Middle East or anywhere else that speculators can take advantage of, prices change in an instant. It's no coincidence Sir Edward and Jim Reegan put their tidy group in Dubai. Being that close to the Persian Gulf and the Straits of Hormuz creates a lot of confidence, which is the same reason they have an Iranian member."

"And the two others connected to your work with the Super PAC—the good one? They eliminated them"

"Yes. They killed them both as well," said Brooks.

"The money the Dubai group discussed from your listening post we tracked from a Swiss account to the Caymans. Everyone they have on the-take is paid as a consultant to dummy companies. Besides that information, you're the only one who heard about the contract killings. I wonder how their new bartender's doing?" Mansfield asked.

Brooks smiled.

"I can't figure out why they just didn't kill me."

"We suspect they placed the ransom on your head to create the look of a small-time group looking for some cash." Mansfield hadn't moved from his perch leaning on the table.

"After I give witness to what I heard and point to faces, I may be done working in the field." Johns Brooks was relieved to say that.

"Don't worry, John. We have a cozy office and promotion already waiting for you."

"How's Ramsey and Moore?" Brooks' affect was sincere.

"It's been nip and tuck a couple times. Ramsey thinks he

knows who he's after. As far as we know, Moore doesn't have a clue." Mansfield sat back in his chair with his shoulders slumped and relaxed.

"He'll figure it out—but back to the money. Who's in the bag?" Brooks tried to sound cavalier about his old partner and informant, but he was worried about them.

"As far as we can tell there are ten senators; twenty-four House members; two Presidential candidates; and, believe it or not, one Justice. Probably a whole slew of staffers." Mansfield was getting restless and he sensed Brooks' mood change. Most everything had been said. "So, what say we get some food?" Jim Mansfield stood up and straightened his crumpled sweater and hitched up his Dockers.

"Sure. I could eat a horse."

"How about we settle for some cafeteria mystery meat instead?"

The two men left the conference room and walked down the hall. People shook Brooks' hand as he passed them by.

Senator David Henry sat back in his Queen Anne's leather chair and looked up at the clock. It was 10:00 a.m. He decided to get some breakfast prior to a late-Friday session. He poked his head into the office in front of his. "Hal, breakfast?"

"Already had mine, but I could go for a second." Hal Barnes was no man to turn down food. Having a short stature, his white shirts were always stretched, and his ties always strained to reach his belt as they curved over his large belly. Barnes fit the prototypical southern political operative mold.

"Order in or downstairs?" Senator Henry put on his sport coat.

"Let's walk. I didn't do my treadmill today. Wait, I haven't done it all year!" Both men laughed.

"Hal, you're too sneaky to be healthy, but you'll outlive us all. Let's go."

They exited the office and headed for the private dining room. There were only a few people who passed them in the hallway.

They took one of the small side stairways. Sometimes the stairs in the Capitol would be jammed with people going up and down, to where you'd have to wait, but this morning the stairwell was empty.

"Anything new about our dead friend?" Senator Henry asked.

"No. The Feds followed something in Texas, but couldn't find anything. They want warrants to clean out files and to search the building. Probably later today or tomorrow." Hal Barnes led the way down the stairs.

"What about … oh, never mind." The good senator remembered the group's oath to only tell staff members what they should know and only then to make sure it was a help and not a hindrance. Hal Barnes had been with him since 1964. Senator Henry felt comfortable the leak wasn't in his office. Only the six members of the Super PAC, a few NSA staff, and the President knew everything. David Henry was anxious for Friday, but more anxious to make sure the two star witnesses made it.

"How long?" Parker asked Rick, the service manager at Brown Motors.

"Maybe an hour. We have everything ready to go, and we're pretty slow today. Need a ride somewhere?"

"No. I'll just sit in the waiting room and write." Parker had his laptop with him. He didn't notice anyone unfamiliar around him and had not seen anyone following him. He left the church at 10:00 a.m. It was now 10:20.

Ramsey was parked a block from her house on Mitchell. Her car was still in the driveway.

"Laura, are you still coming in today?" Rocco was seeing patients at the clinic as fast as he could. The front desk was falling behind with patients coming and going.

"Yeah. Yeah. I told them I would be in around ten thirty. I'm just getting ready to leave." Laura looked in the mirror to make any last-minute adjustments to her hair.

"Good, because we're swamped. Get your butt in here." Rocco hung up.

"I'm so glad this is my last day," Laura said as she calmly walked out the side door of the rental house and into her car.

"Is everybody where they should be?" asked Tim Johnson.

"Yup. Some are tired, but they're in position." Pete Stuart sat in a red MacGregor's Plumbing and Heating van in the Glen's Market parking lot near the Crest View clinic. "Two of 'em are on the roof working on the heating and air conditioning units. I hope they don't break the damn things."

"The others?" Johnson was at Parker Moore's house, staring out the front door at the empty white van.

"All set."

"Good. I'll stay here to make sure somebody sees me here. Sure hope this works. I want my quiet town back." He clicked off.

Pete Stuart stepped out of the van looking the part in his MacGregor uniform. He had known the MacGregor family for years; they were up for anything to help the state police catch a bad guy. Stuart and his two fellow officers picked up three vans after they made sure Parker got to the church safely. The one officer in the chapel said all was well once Parker left for Brown Motors. No sign of anyone suspicious.

The director had just put his phone in his pocket when it rang again. He continued to look out the window of the front door. "Johnson."

"Tim, when do I get the story about the guy in that house on Mitchell? All I've printed so far is what you told me about the same guy who they thought had a heart attack at that same address a few days before. That's too much action for one sick bastard. Oh, and about the morgue guy found shot ... We have to sell papers, you know." It was Harvey Snow from the *Petoskey News and Review.*

"Harvey, if everything happens that I think might happen, you'll be at *The New York Times* very soon."

"Tim, I could give a rat's ass about *The New York Times.* I'm too old for that bullshit. And you're giving me bullshit. But, I'm a trooper and will go along for the good of the cause. I just want a story." Harvey was pleading.

"Harvey, you'll get it. Just not right now."

32

Two men stood in front of his desk. "Yes, yes, can I help you?" asked the Dubai merchant. He wore a navy blue suit with large shiny stripes. His white shirt and pink tie finished off a loud ensemble.

"Yes," said the man wearing a gray suit. "You arrange for people to find employment in American and European offices or businesses?"

"Yes. I do. Please, is there a need?"

"Actually," the man in a tan suit walked closer to the flashy merchant, "we're here to take over your business." He stuck out a TASER M26C; the merchant buckled and dropped into the arms of the man in the gray suit.

Another man in jeans and a white buttoned shirt came in with a shopping bag. Inside was a body bag. The merchant's striped suit clashed with the gray interior of the body bag, but that didn't prevent the men from zipping the bag and carrying it to a van that was backed right up to the twin glass doors. In a span of two minutes the body was removed and all three men and the bag were gone.

It was 7:30 p.m. in Dubai. The group had reassembled for the last night of their meetings. The new bartender carried a tray of martinis around. Jim Reegan looked at the bartender and stopped him. "Did you come from the agency?"

"Yes, sir. I'm a doctoral student in Middle Eastern Studies and the cousin of ..." he stopped and looked around. Bending over to where Jim Reegan was sitting, the bartender whispered a name into Reegan's ear.

"Oh. Okay then. I'll have a bourbon. Neat." He let go of the bartender's arm.

The Norwegian woman and the Russian businessman sat on the large brown-leather sofa talking about the new pipeline from Azerbaijan. Sir Edward held a Tanqueray martini while he stood near the window looking out at the Persian Gulf. Next to him were a Canadian gentleman and the newest member from Iran.

"Sir Edward, are we to understand that our last deposits have been accounted for and sent along for their intended purpose?" asked the Canadian.

"Most assuredly. We've also been informed that the cap-and-trade legislation in the U.S. House has been halted in committee." Sir Edward turned around to answer and smile before turning back toward the window.

The ten people soon found their way toward the center of the room into the soft leather furniture that formed a wide circle. Dinner was being served one at a time by the bartender onto small tables set before each person in a very informal fashion.

"Please, eat. We'll complete our discussions after dinner. Enjoy." Sir Edward sat with the others and began to cut into his rare filet mignon. As he chewed the succulent steak, he glanced at Reegan who was getting a second bourbon and checking his watch.

"So, what do you think will happen at the committee meeting, David?" Hal Barnes picked up a slice of bacon with his fingers and put it in his mouth.

"Not sure, Hal. Not sure." David Henry's chief of staff knew most everything, but Barnes didn't know who was being called as witnesses at the not-yet-public meeting.

"By the way, who are the special folks you're waiting for?" Barnes was now forking eggs into his mouth.

"Just some witnesses we've been wanting to talk to. Nothing major."

"Then why the secrecy?" Barnes had stopped shoveling food and was getting a little perturbed that he was being left out of the loop.

"Just be patient. You'll be there. Let's just call it a surprise." Henry smiled and tried to be nonchalant as he dabbled with his eggs. He grabbed some toast and looked into his friend's eyes as he took his last bite. "Look at the time. We must get upstairs." Senator Henry wiped his mouth with his napkin and placed it on top of his plate as he stood up.

The two men left the dining room. After a couple hallway conversations, they finally made their way back into the Senate Minority Office.

It was 11:55 a.m.

33

"Moore? Parker Moore?" The service manager called Parker's name.

"Here I am." Parker's big frame was crunched into one of the waiting room chairs, and he hung over his laptop as it sat on his knees.

"Good news and bad news. The reason it took so long was because your rotors were shot on the back wheels. We did your rear brakes as well since you told us to fix anything that needed fixing." The service manager was looking at his clipboard as he spoke.

"All right. Guess I'll settle up." Parker looked at his watch and was stunned to see it was after noon. He got up and made his way to the cashier. After paying for the parts and service, he walked out through the garage to his car. As he went out the rear door, the mechanics' coats were all lined up. There was a tan Carhartt coat exactly like the one he'd seen before.

Laura was at her desk catching up on the medical record coding. She noticed several workers gathered outside the office and looking at the roof from the parking lot. One man kept looking at her. "What the hell do you want?" she said out loud. She picked up the phone.

Parker was preoccupied by the coat. As soon as he drove away, he started to talk (Stuart had wired Parker before he left home). "Guys, I don't know who's listening to me, but the Carhartt coat was hanging at the dealership. So far, the car's fine."

Ramsey heard everything. "Got it, Parker. We'll check it out."

The voice in Parker's ear made him jump. "Ramsey, you scared the shit outta me!" Parker was smiling though, and he instantly felt better. He had no idea where Ramsey was. He noticed his phone vibrate as it rested in the cup holder behind the gear shift next to his right thigh.

"Parker? When the hell are you coming over? I need a ride to Conway." The men outside were irritating Laura.

"On my way now. Everything okay?" he answered.

"No. I got here late, there are men on the roof messing with the heat, and I have to get to Conway to pick up a box of medical records." At six foot one in flats and a perfect size seven, Laura was an intimidating presence, but she was generally soft with Parker. (She always had other intentions for him.)

"I can pick those up." Parker was watching the traffic as he made his way south on US-31 through the Chautauqua community of Bay View. The fall fury of the Great Lakes was missing today. Lake Michigan had only a few ripples from the westerly breeze.

"No. I need a break from this place and you're going to take me. Especially after that miserable date last night—or whatever it was." Laura looked up at the clock.

"Fine. Be there in ten minutes. Any clients for me today?"

"No. Thus the reason you're taking me to Conway. Duh." Laura hung up.

"Ramsey, I'm going to Conway sooner than normal," he said.

"We got ya, Parker." Ramsey answered back into the earpiece.

Parker turned on the CD player and picked number four. George Winston's Fall came over the speakers. He first bought the album as a cassette in 1980. It was on a trip north with his father, when they first bought the property on the river. The music always brought back good memories in tough times. Parker kept wishing he'd live long enough to spend the rest of his days at that cabin looking over the high bank of the Manistee River. In an instant, the stress of the day melted away.

As he made his way through the bit of traffic Petoskey had, he came up on the hospital and then past the corner where US-31 turned west toward Charlevoix. He continued south on what was now US-131 toward the Kmart plaza known as Crest View Mall. In the rearview mirror he saw a midnight blue Suburban. It looked like one of the SUVs the President of the United States would have in his cavalcade.

"Is that you behind me?" Parker wondered if people around him would think he was nuts talking to himself.

"Shhh. You're not supposed to see me," Ramsey answered back laughing.

"It's tough when you drive a bus like that."

"Yeah. Well, I saw enough of these up here that I didn't think it looked out of the ordinary." Ramsey had picked up the SUV at Exports, Inc. located at Pellston Airport. Exports, Inc. only existed on paper.

"So, if we keep hooking up like this, do I eventually get an Austin Martin or maybe a Ferrari?" Parker was calmer than he thought. The familiar feeling of confidence that all would be okay hovered around him. He was a firm believer in auras and liked the one he was feeling.

"No."

"That seems to be the answer of the day."

The fifth track played as Parker drove up the hill to Sheridan and merged into the left-hand turn lane. The navy blue SUV passed on his right. The driver's window was blackened. He never saw Ramsey.

34

Two men in suits entered the elevator of the high-rise. A man in jeans and a white oxford shirt accompanied them into the building, but he remained on the first floor and walked toward a door marked Security. Their name tags identified them as guests from Exports, Inc. The suits made their way to the near top of 23 Marina, one of seventeen skyscrapers in Dubai taller than 300 meters; this one was the tallest residential building in the world. One of the newest buildings nearby pierced the sky more than a half mile into the air.

As the two men exited the elevator into the glass-lined hallway on the 88th floor, two shy of the top, they worked their way toward the large suite that blocked the hallway and another elevator entry. There were two emergency doors that only opened out. Above them was a vent that led to the private elevator shaft in the private suite. So far, the details John Brooks provided in his debriefing were perfect.

"Now," whispered one of the men; the hallway camera stopped working.

They popped the vent, and one man hoisted the other into the ceiling space.

"Rocco, how's business today?" Parker had just arrived at the Crest View Clinic.

"Good. It's my last day though. My wife's been busy packing.

You wanna catch a drink later?" Rocco was walking into a treatment room.

"Last day?"

"Yes. The regular therapy staff will be back next week, and I have another assignment." Rocco was matter-of-fact.

"Where are you headed?" Parker was curious. So many new people; he looked at everyone with suspicion.

"Out of the country. A dream come true." Rocco entered the treatment room and closed the door.

Parker watched the door close.

"Wasn't your Carhartt, Parker. The mechanic has been there for twenty years. Stay on your path." Ramsey chimed into Parker's ear as Parker walked to the rear of the clinic to check the mailboxes.

"Moore? You ready?" Laura was putting on her coat.

"Yeah, sure. Let me see if there's anything that needs to go to the other clinics." Parker walked in the back room. Rocco's Carhartt hung on the coatrack. "Geez. Does everybody own one of these?"

All of the mailboxes were empty, so Parker returned to the clinic area. Laura was standing at the counter. Her long wool coat was unbuttoned and Parker couldn't help but notice her long slit skirt that suggestively revealed her long legs as she leaned on the counter with her elbow. Her blouse was open to her cleavage and her hair had never looked so perfect.

"Ready?" Parker asked as he stepped toward the door.

"More than ready. Are you?" She smiled and grabbed Parker's tie, pulling him out the door.

Pete Stuart and the other two shadows were by the MacGregor's Plumbing and Heating vans in the lot near Parker's car.

"You growing a beard, Moore?" Laura said as she got into Parker's car.

"A beard? No. Just haven't shaved in a while. Thought I'd take on that metro-sexual look."

"Yeah, that works in Petoskey," Laura said as she rolled her eyes and looked out the side window at the three plumbers. They were looking at what appeared to be a schematic diagram. She smiled and waved at them. The men never looked up until Parker drove past them.

"He's out of the nest," Pete Stuart said.

It was 12:30 p.m.

"It's getting past nine thirty, and since this is the last evening of our quarterly meeting, let me give a summary of how our money has been used up to this point." Sir Edward was sitting in one of the sofas surrounded by the other nine members of the super PAC he and Jim Reegan formed five years ago.

The night in Dubai was clear and a pleasant sixty-seven degrees. The morning fog was long gone, thus they had a spectacular view. The fog was expected to return by morning; however, the visitors planned on leaving before then. Private and charter flights had been arranged; some even by government agencies of their countries.

"First, we've made sure there will be no trans-Canada pipeline to Texas. We've been assured Iran will continue to float the story of removing their oil from the world market and, the best news of all, our largest bank in the room topped 1.2 trillion dollars in returns after the bailout. Thank you, Mr. Landau." Sir Edward nodded at Jonathan Landau, president of the largest banking house in the United States. "Therefore, we will continue our pressure on the U.S. system to keep the current banking structure intact. There were some fines paid by Mr. Landau's group—but as the Americans say on, is it ESPN?—thank you for taking one for the team." He chuckled.

"Now, on another matter, we continue to win on the Kyoto front. Canada is backing out since their emissions actually have been rising. More fuel, more money, and control for us." Sir Edward looked around the room until he stopped on the Canadian representative, then he moved his glance to the Russian member. "Mr. Egorov has continued to make Kyoto somewhat perplexing since Russia, which is the world's largest producer, has to pay or change nothing. Our continued thanks to you, Evgeny."

Evgeny Egorov, holder of the most oil and gas properties in

Russia, toasted Sir Edward and the others with his vodka. "It's been a most pleasurable experience."

"Sir Edward?" Jim Reegan chimed in.

"Yes, Mr. Reegan, the floor is yours."

Jim Reegan stood and walked over to the bar to refresh his bourbon. "We're working on our next scenario, which is the fracking issue in the United States. Other less-regulated countries are pulling this off without difficulty. We're at a crossroads as to whether we should be on the pro or con side of this subject in America. The more difficult it is to accomplish, the prices we hold dear continue to be high. If the pressure eases, some small operators gain market share in natural gas and we have yet to acquire some of those holdings. If it pleases the group, we can present a plan at the next meeting." Jim Reegan continued to stand behind the sofas.

The group members turned to each other in small discussions of hushed tones.

Sir Edward spoke. "It sounds as if that would be fine, Mr. Reegan. Right? Now, are there any other items for our agenda—or any questions?" Sir Edward finished his port. "Fine. Safe travels to all, and thank you. Mr. Reegan, a word with you after?"

Reegan shook the men's hands and kissed the women's cheeks as they waited near the elevator. Sir Edward was directly across from him doing the same. The elevator arrived and the eight members worked their way in. The elevator made its way down the private elevator shaft without difficulty or hesitation.

The bartender approached and asked Sir Edward and Reegan if there were any last requests.

"One more Maker's, thank you."

"Hendricks neat, please, kind sir."

Sir Edward made his way to the window. Jim Reegan stood next to him.

On his way to the bar, the bartender reached over and hit the button to return the elevator.

"Has our issue been resolved yet, Mr. Reegan?" Sir Edward stared out the window, taking in the view of the gulf.

"I've been assured by 6:00 p.m. Eastern Standard Time our issue will be taken care of."

"Right. Oh, thank you." Sir Edward turned and received his drink.

Reegan took his glass of whiskey. The bartender retreated to his enclave.

"To the 2012 elections." Sir Edward reached his glass over to Reegan, standing on his right.

"To the elections." Jim Reegan reached across his body with his drink waist high and they quietly but confidently clinked glasses.

The men downed their drinks in one gulp.

"Shall we?" Sir Edward pointed with his empty glass toward the elevator.

"Yes. Let's get out of here before the morning fog."

The elevator had returned to the 88th floor. To hold it, the bartender pushed the hold button. There was no alarm. He looked up and saw that the elevator escape hatch above the decorative light array in the ceiling was ajar.

After the men placed their glasses on the bar, they made their way to the elevator. The bartender was waiting with his gloved hands folded just below his belt. He politely gestured with his right hand for the men to enter. He smiled as the men nodded.

"Good night, gentleman. Safe travels." He pulled out the hold button, and the doors began to close.

It was just after 11:00 p.m. in Dubai.

35

Jim Mansfield, NSA Director of Field Agents, was waiting for FBI Special Agent Jack Fletcher inside the front door of the NSA headquarters in Fort Meade, Maryland. He looked at the clock. It was 2:05 p.m. He noticed a gentleman wearing a black suit walk in and look around like he'd never been there before.

"Fletcher?" Mansfield stuck out his right hand.

"Director Mansfield." Jack Fletcher grabbed the hand and shook it firmly.

"Let's get you checked through security."

The two men cleared their credentials and waited for the elevator. Mansfield was dressed in tan Dockers and a dark blue polo shirt covered by a brown cardigan sweater. He stood next to the impeccably dressed Special Agent who yawned.

"Coffee? I assume you've had lunch." Mansfield sized up Fletcher as he talked.

"Please. It was a longer drive than I thought," said Fletcher. Little affect showed through his facial expressions.

The elevator opened and the two walked in. Several others were also present, so there was quiet. Fletcher was overdressed compared to the NSA employees in casual clothes, but it didn't bother him. He just stared up at the floor numbers as they dinged by.

"Here we go, Jack." Mansfield shifted his way through the crowd and led Fletcher down the hall toward his fourth-floor office. As they passed the secretary's office, Mansfield poked his head in. "Can you get us a couple of coffees?" He paused and looked at Fletcher.

"Black for me."

"Both black. Thanks, Kirk. Just bring them in when you get back." Mansfield opened his office door and closed it behind him after Fletcher slowly entered. The office was bland, with a few plaques and certificates on the walls. The desk top and adjoining table were covered with research materials: papers, books, newspapers. In the middle of it all was Mansfield's laptop.

"Sorry about the mess. Here, let me clear you a spot." Mansfield grunted as he reached over the table and took off some papers and books.

Fletcher sat down. "Maid due?"

"No. We've cut back. We only get manicures and valet parking. The office dump is left to us." Mansfield smiled. Fletcher didn't.

There was still no pertinent discussion. Fletcher sat there stoically. He figured it was Mansfield's show, so he could start. The director finally found his well-worn high-back leather chair and sat down with a thud and a sigh. The armrests were rubbed down to the metal where Mansfield placed his hands; he had them covered with duct tape.

"Agent Fletcher, Jack, I'd like to update you on the Fairchild case and the connected issues with Petoskey, Michigan." Mansfield had several maps out on his desk and several close-up shots of Parker Moore's house and neighborhood. There were also memos concerning phone calls and text messages in the area over a two-week time span. There was one message on a plain white sheet of paper from Todd Ramsey that contained one name.

Jack Fletcher's brow was furrowed. His face finally showed some emotion. It was frustration short of anger. In the last twenty-four hours, he'd been informed both dead men connected with the case were missing. He was given what he thought was misleading information about a security company that had been purchased by an oil and gas conglomerate in Texas. His men looked like fools rushing in and finding nothing. He sat with his right elbow on the table and his hand holding his chin with his index finger rubbing back and forth above his top lip.

"I'm waiting," he said.

"There's a lot you don't know, and I'm sure it's been frustrating. But it's time we brought you up to speed. Once I explain everything to you, you'll feel better—I hope. Plus, we now need your help for the public side of this."

Mansfield got up and brought an armful of notes and pictures and placed them in front of Fletcher. He powered up the laptop and turned it around to face both men. Mansfield stood over Fletcher and pointed to the desk. "Here's where we're at."

The knock at the door brought Mansfield's personal assistant, Kirk, into the room with the coffee.

"Thanks, Kirk. Can you get me the latest from Dubai and bring that in as well?" Mansfield smiled and Kirk left, shutting the door behind him.

36

Pete Stuart looked at his watch. It was 2:30 p.m. He and his fellow shadows were doing what they thought real heating and cooling workers would do while they kept their eyes open for the person Todd Ramsey said they should be looking for. The other two people of interest were already in the clinic. One just drove away.

Another MacGregor truck was at the Conway clinic. A ladder leading up to the roof stood by the birdfeeders at the side entrance. On the roof, a shadow dressed in MacGregor overalls was wrenching on the pipes to the heating system. The clinic staff had looked at the work order and all seemed to be in order. Forged signature and all.

At the Harbor Springs clinic, the MacGregor pickup was parked in front of the Dollar Store. The MacGregor shop was right around the corner from the clinic and Dollar Store, so nothing seemed out of place. The driver of the pickup watched the comings and goings of the staff and clients from the roof of the strip mall across the street.

Todd Ramsey followed Parker Moore's car while the two occupants ran their errands and stopped for gas. Finally, at 2:35 p.m., the silver Fusion entered the Conway clinic parking lot. Ramsey was about two hundred yards and two cars behind the Fusion, heading east on Conway Road, but with the height of the Suburban, Ramsey could see where Parker's car turned.

"So, Gwen, anything today? Clients? Mail?" Although Parker was confident, there was also some healthy anxiety in carting around Laura. He smiled when he spoke to Gwen.

"No new clients. These envelopes need to go to Harbor." Gwen spun her chair around from the front glass window view to Parker at the other end of her desk. She looked past Parker to Laura who was standing at the door.

"Charts? I'm here for the charts?" Laura leaned against the doorjamb.

"Oh, yeah, the charts." said Gwen as she looked at Laura.

Parker noticed the look. He noticed everything today; he felt the hackles on the back of his neck stand up.

Gwen got up from her chair and walked around back to the kitchen storage area. Laura followed. As Parker turned to follow them, he noticed the blue Suburban parked across the street in a storage garage parking lot. With the other trucks around, the only noticeable difference was the blackened windows.

"Here, Parker. Some fresh coffee." Laura handed Parker a cup as he turned the corner around the cubicle that led to the kitchen.

"Ah, thanks, Laura." Parker took it as Laura turned back and headed into the kitchen. He didn't drink any of it, and continued to walk to the kitchen.

"Here's the box of records. It's pretty heavy, so be careful, Parker." Gwen was standing next to the counter with her legs crossed as she leaned her shoulder on the top cupboard. The box was at her feet. It was a standard brown document file box with a lid that was taped so as not to come off.

Parker put the coffee cup down and bent over to grab the box. Gwen never moved as he brushed against her leg. He tried not to look at the length of her legs as he lifted the box. Laura was next to him and bent over with him. She checked the tape on the box as Parker stood with it.

"I got this, ladies." He looked at one then the other as they stood on either side of him. Gwen was as tall as Laura and at forty-two, still a svelte size seven. Both women were smiling. "Um, can I get these out to the car?"

"Sure, Parker." Laura moved ever so slightly to allow Parker to exit the kitchen. Gwen never moved. Her expression never changed.

As Parker left the kitchen, Laura turned and put her thumbs up to Gwen.

Ramsey heard the kitchen conversation and then watched Parker carry out the taped box. His senses began to heighten. He knew the time was at hand, and he was convinced there would be an attempt on Moore's life within the next few hours. The only question was who was going to do it. There were three possibilities. Distractions were becoming more intense. The scenario with the two women in the kitchen could have been a diversion. What was in the box? As Parker's car pulled up the hill and out of the driveway westbound on Conway Road, Ramsey waited until they crested another hill by the BP gas station before he turned out behind them. He heard nothing in his earpiece from Parker's car, but the laptop affixed to the dashboard showed the silver Fusion traveling as it should toward Harbor Springs.

The weather was turning. The plush fall clouds earlier in the day were darkening over the lake and moving inward. The sun was gone and a light rain scattered mist across the horizon.

It was 3:05 p.m.

37

"Mr. President, motion to adjourn," Senator Henry announced.

"Hearing no objection ..." the Vice President of the United States, serving as the President of the Senate, paused. "This session stands adjourned." The gavel rang down.

Senator Henry quickly made his way to the lobby directly to the right of the Senate President's seat. Both men walked toward the formal office of the Vice President.

"Mr. Vice President, I wanted to let you know we're following through with our discussion. The Intelligence Committee will meet Friday afternoon in an emergency session."

"Okay. Are we ready for all of the outcomes?" Vice President Russell was sitting and tying his shoe. He looked up and sat back in the wooden chair. His arms hung down, palms out. He rested his head back on the ancient oak of the chair back. After a deep breath, he said, "If this happens as we've planned, our government will never be the same."

"Harry, we don't want it to be the same, and we certainly don't want other countries with business PACs running it." Senator David Henry had his game face on. He was standing a few feet from the Vice President and his affect was just short of angry. "You know what's at stake here. You know this is a bipartisan agenda that will give the people back their government. If it doesn't, God help us."

"I know, David. I know." Harry Russell composed himself and sat straight up in the chair. "We'll meet in the Oval Office at seven. I'm going to go have a stiff drink. Care to join me?" The Vice President stood and looked in the mirror to straighten his tie.

"No, thanks. I still have a leak, and am afraid if I deviate from the script of the day … well, let's just say I could put the entire mission in jeopardy. I'll see you later. And, Harry? Thanks." Senator Henry turned and left the office.

Hal Barnes was waiting for the senator in the hallway. "What was that all about?" Hal Barnes walked just behind the senator as he shuffled some papers to the top of the stack he held in both hands.

"He just wanted an update on Mark Fairchild's death. I told him the FBI was working the case, and the only lead we had in Texas turned out to be false."

"False? Where next?" Barnes stopped shuffling papers. He was sweating at his brow, thanks in part to all the weight he was carrying around. He took one of the papers and wiped the sweat away. "Geez, I really need to—" He fell flat on his face.

"Hal? HAL!?" Senator Henry stopped, turned around, and quickly came to the side of his fallen aide. His best friend for fifty years.

"I'm okay. I'm okay." Barnes was trying to get to his knees. He couldn't stop shaking. "I think it's my blood sugar. Just get me up and get me some orange juice."

The two men struggled to get Barnes to the closest chair in the hallway. He sat down with a flop. Senator Henry picked up a house phone and called for assistance.

"David, I just want you to know how much I've loved working with you all these years—but the stress of this is going to kill me." Tears welled up in Hal Barnes' eyes.

"Hal, what is it?" As Senator Henry knelt down and looked his friend in the eyes, the Capitol Police and rescue personnel came running down the hall. They arrived before Barnes was able to respond. Senator Henry just stepped back and watched.

"So, we make all of the arrests when?" Jack Fletcher stood at the window of John Mansfield's office with his hands on his hips.

He noticed the fall colors were bright with reds and oranges. There was a slight breeze through the trees; it was a cool fifty-eight degrees outside. Fletcher had his coat off and sleeves rolled up. His tie was hanging over the back of one of the chairs at the table. Papers and maps were scattered about even more so than before. Some were on the floor around the chair where Jack Fletcher had been sitting. "And how in the hell do we—"

"Jack, it's not going to be exactly like that. There will be investigations. Lawyers. More investigations and more lawyers—but the fact remains, these people won't win their re-elections. There may only be the few arrests this weekend." John Mansfield looked disheveled. His sweater sleeves were at different lengths on his arms. His thin hair was arranged at different angles from his fingers combing through it. "We're telling you this so as not to alert your bosses before we have to. There is a leak and we're not taking any chances. You can go where we need you in connection to the Fairchild case without looking any different to your superiors. After all, that is your case."

Jack Fletcher turned around and kept his left hand on his hip while his right hand came up and rubbed his forehead. "And, again, where are the two key witnesses?"

"One is surrounded by U.S. Marshals in an undisclosed location, and the other is running around Petoskey, Michigan, trying to stay alive so we can trap the security company."

"So, how do you know I'm not the leak?" Jack Fletcher walked to his chair and sat down. He actually looked and acted more relaxed than when he came into the office.

"Jack. We're the NSA. We know. We know." Mansfield rested his forearms on his desk with his hands folded. "Hell, we just need to hold our breath for the next few hours. We had to be so careful with this group. Their reach is enormous." He sat back in his chair and clasped his hands behind his head. "At one point, we questioned each other, so there were only a couple agents; no elaborate measures for people to find and track. It's been like the days of the Cold War. Your agency tends to be so public, we had to wait till everything fell into place. Now, we wait to see if the American people will believe digital voice recordings and two witnesses who can put two men in the same place at the same time talking about manipulating the American government through a political action committee anointed by our wonderful Supreme Court."

"Will we get to see the six people in the Super PAC?" Fletcher asked.

"No," Mansfield said without hesitation.

"Why didn't the leak just pull a WikiLeak job on them?"

"Because, Agent Fletcher, people would begin to ask questions, and the big question would be why we have our own Super PAC; the trillions of dollars being stockpiled to influence our Presidential election might up-and-disappear before we nab the bad guys. Besides, we assume the leak only knows about the Stimson connection and that someone's had a hard-on to solve it. That's why we kept pointing them your way." Mansfield stood up slowly. "Let's call it a day. When you get back, you can meet the witnesses and we'll chat again."

Jack Fletcher didn't move. He looked like he'd seen a ghost. "Get back? Get back from where?"

John Brooks sat in his room at the Navy Lodge in Annapolis, Maryland, with three U.S. Marshals watching FOX News. Someone turned the channel to MSNBC.

"Hey, don't you believe what their saying?" Brooks said from the sofa. His legs stretched out over the coffee table.

"Saying? None of them say anything. I look for the shortest skirts," said the Deputy Marshal in the Lazy Boy. The whole group laughed.

John Brooks glanced at his watch. It was 3:30 p.m. He wondered what Todd Ramsey was doing to keep Parker Moore alive.

38

"Parker, pull over there for a minute." Laura pointed to the park across from Bay Bluffs, just before the road heads downhill into Harbor Springs.

"Why? I really shouldn't." Parker's nerves were peaking. He would usually be at the Harbor clinic for his last stop before returning to Petoskey; then at the gym by 4:30.

"Parker, give me fifteen minutes. It's my last day," Laura pleaded. The slit in her skirt revealed most of her inner thighs.

As Parker turned the car into the park, Ramsey drove into Bay Bluffs and parked in the front lot. Parker's car came to a rest under a tree parallel to the bluff. The thinning trees allowed a view of Little Traverse Bay from the bluff side of Harbor Springs.

Laura reached around to the backseat and opened the box. Parker couldn't believe what he saw.

Pete Stuart was getting restless. The men sat in their vans and ate lunch. One by one, they would take turns to climb back on the roof.

"Nothing yet, Ramsey. Can we let the truck at Conway join us?" Stuart's eyes were glued to the clinic entrance.

"Yes. Conway is off the grid. Bring him in," Ramsey replied as he looked through the scope into Parker's car. He smiled. Laura lifted out a bottle of wine, two glasses, and some bread and cheese from the box.

He listened to the conversation.

"Parker, you have a way about you. I know you're married and all, but one small minute with me isn't going to hurt anyone. Sam's gone. I'll be gone. It'll be like it never happened. We can start here and finish at my place. Gwen said she might even join us." Laura was slowly unbuttoning her blouse.

"Laura, look. I don't do this anymore. There was a time when I wasn't as careful, but not now and not ever again." Parker could only imagine what Ramsey was thinking.

"Parker, you gotta get out of this. We're gonna save you, but Sam will kill you if this keeps going," Ramsey said into Parker's ear.

Laura nuzzled Parker's right ear while he held the glass of wine. Is this it? Is this part of the plot? he wondered.

Ramsey called Director Johnson.

Laura was unzipping Parker's pants. He looked like a nervous teenager at his first drive-in movie with a date. She, on the other hand, was a professional.

"I make a mark, Parker, at each one of my assignments. It's kind of a game. I tagged you from the beginning."

Before Parker could completely lose himself, or grab her hand and get out of the car, a Harbor Springs Police car pulled into the west entrance of the park. Parker saw it in the rearview mirror.

"Laura, really, this isn't going to work. Besides, we have company."

She quickly looked up and out the back window and saw the fully marked Malibu slowing to a stop. In one swift motion, she closed her legs, buttoned her blouse and sat up straight. The wine hadn't been poured, but the crackers and cheese sat on the center console.

"Shit, of all the ..." Laura was angry.

"I know him. We'll be okay." Parker arranged himself and opened the window to greet the Chief of Police, Pat Sutherland.

Parker poked his head out.

"Moore? Is that you?" Sutherland took his hand off the top of his weapon and stood directly in front of the window.

"Yes, Pat. This is Laura. She's one of our staff at the clinics, and since this is her last day, well, she was trying to make it one to remember." Parker turned his now angry gaze at Laura as she sat staring out the windshield.

"Hello, Chief. Parker, can we just move on?"

"Laura." The chief tipped his hat. "Moore, don't let me stop you, if this is what you want. As long as that wine isn't open, you're okay here." Sutherland was smiling broadly. He couldn't wait to call Tim Johnson back and tell him what he found.

"No. No. Thanks for the offer, Chief, but we need to move on. I'll just drive over to the clinic."

Ramsey laughed quietly in Parker's ear. "Sorry, Parker. I guess she's not the one." He continued to laugh.

"See ya soon, Moore. Tell Sam I said hello." The chief backed up as Parker shifted the car into drive.

"Sure. Yeah. I'll tell her," Parker said quietly as he rolled up the window and waved to Pat Sutherland in the mirror. He turned the car out onto M-119.

Laura pulled out a cigarette.

"No smoking in the car, Laura." Parker turned the car onto Lake Street.

"Kiss my ass, Moore. Suddenly I can't keep any guy interested. I still don't know what happened to Mr. Carhartt." Laura rolled down her window and let the smoke blow out. The mist over the water had made its way inland; the cooling breeze helped detract her embarrassment and frustration.

Todd Ramsey gave them a few minutes then put the Harbor clinic MacGregor truck on alert. The shadow was now in the truck drinking coffee and reading the paper. No one fitting the description of Ramsey's other suspect had arrived.

The silver Fusion pulled into the Fairview Mall lot; pulling in right behind the Fusion, a silver minivan parked on the opposite side of the lot. The Harbor clinic sat nestled in the corner of the mall. Ramsey was parked in the rear of the adjoining mall across the street facing Meyer's Ace Hardware. He watched Rocco, wearing his tan Carhartt coat, step out of the van and walk toward the clinic. Both of his hands were in his coat pockets.

Even though Parker had parked in the farthest corner of the lot, so as not to disturb patients who wanted to be near the front door, Rocco saw Parker and Laura. He immediately turned around and began to walk toward them.

The MacGregor man was pretending to adjust something in the bed of the pickup—in actuality, he held a .9mm Glock under a towel. Rocco was only four feet behind him. Todd Ramsey had already mounted his rifle and was following Rocco in the scope.

Laura exited the car first and ran to Rocco. Parker slowly closed the door and looked over at Ramsey's Suburban, then the shadow at the MacGregor truck. When Laura reached Rocco, she grabbed him and whispered something in his ear. He smiled and continued to walk toward Parker. Laura continued into the clinic. As Rocco neared Parker, the MacGregor shadow slowly brought his gun up to a level just below the top of the truck bed. Ramsey's trigger was being lightly feathered by his right index finger. The scope and sight in line with Rocco's head dead center.

39

"Rocco." Parker pushed at his coat pocket. He wished he'd grabbed the Chief's Special.

"Moore." Rocco brought his hands out of the pockets of his coat. They were empty. He reached out to shake Parker's hand. "I just wanted to say good-bye. This assignment has been great, and I hope you don't mind being a reference for me down the road." Rocco's face was sincerely happy.

"No. No problem." Parker felt the wind leave his sails. His hand was shaking as Rocco grabbed it.

The MacGregor man returned his weapon to the back of his pants and covered it with his coat. Todd Ramsey took a deep breath but did not put the rifle down. He continued to sight Rocco.

Parker and Rocco turned and went into the clinic. The MacGregor man walked in behind them with his orders in hand—to look at the heating system of the pool.

"Strike two, Parker. We're down to one," Ramsey said into Parker's ear.

Tim Johnson was calm but calculating. It was the best rest he'd had all week, but he continued to trace the scenario of the day through his mind. He also wondered where Jack Fletcher and the FBI had disappeared to. He sat enjoying Parker's media room while watching the street and a house up the hill and across Mitchell. He helped himself to coffee, cookies, listened to some jazz, and treated himself to a Humphrey Bogart theater day on Turner Classic Movies. *The Maltese Falcon* was currently playing. Sam Spade had just found out his partner, Miles Archer, was gunned down in the middle of the night. Probably not the best movie for the situation, but it passed the time.

Johnson peered out the window at a low-profile angle. The car he'd been watching was backing down the driveway. He called Ramsey.

"The car you asked me to watch is leaving as we speak. Can't see inside yet. Looks like whoever it is will be going south on Lockwood. Nope, they're coming this way, down Mitchell. They'll see me in the chair watching TV. Yes. All of the vans and the Malibu are out front. There it goes. A white Audi. West on Mitchell, and it's, hold on, I couldn't see who was driving. Another car passed in front. It might have been two people."

"Give it a few minutes; then take your car to the Crest View Mall by way of Sheridan. Thanks, Tim."

Ramsey stayed where he was until he felt comfortable about Rocco. The MacGregor shadow hadn't yet come out nor had Moore.

Pete Stuart saw Tim Johnson's car pull into the Crest View Mall between Garfield's restaurant and Glen's Market grocery store. Johnson parked in a row of cars near Pier One. He didn't see the white Audi pull into the Kmart lot behind him from US-131. The other two shadows were on the roof and also watching Johnson's car.

The Audi drove to the parking spots that faced Glen's but were above the lower lot. The person in the car had a clear view of everything and everyone.

"Hey, Moore, I'm staying here for a while. Rocco will give me a ride back." Laura sat at the front counter by a spare computer away from the receptionist.

"Why? Something wrong?" Parker would rather be alone, but he was trying to be polite.

"Yes. Complete embarrassment. You take care." Laura's eyes never left the computer screen.

"Okay. See, ya." Parker walked out the door and into the mist. It was after 4:00 p.m. He was late on his rounds.

He walked to his car, glancing across the street to note Ramsey's truck. He got inside and sat for a moment. He set his briefcase in the backseat next to the open box with the spontaneous picnic still intact. For a moment he thought how nice it would be to open the wine and just stay where he was.

"Get moving, Parker. You're behind." Ramsey was in his ear again.

"Are we now looking for the last person on the list?" he asked in return.

"Yup. Head for Petoskey. No stops. Everyone is where they're supposed to be.

Johnson looked at his watch. He thought Parker would be here by now. Since he was too recognizable, Johnson stayed inside the car parked between the trucks. He was driving his wife's Ford Five Hundred. The black paint was tough in the summer, but absorbed all the sun's warmth in the deep of winter. On the passenger seat sat his cell phone, prep radio, and an earpiece—all in working order. He moved his head a little to the left to see around the rearview mirror. As he put in his earpiece, he noticed one man coming down a ladder.

"Sarge, six o'clock, directly behind you. One woman in a white Audi." The shadow was talking as he came down the ladder with his back to the parking lot.

His partner on the roof calmly grabbed some tools and headed for the heating unit above the Kmart store.

Off the ladder, the shadow met Stuart as he exited his vehicle; neither looked back at the Audi. Instead, the two men pointed at the heating unit where their partner was.

"Take the long toolbox with the weapon, and go back up that ladder like it was your best friend. Calmly tell Jim to look at the unit on top of Kmart while you point, and then both of you walk over there. Look busy but disappear behind it and set your sights. This is it." As Pete Stuart talked softly, he never stopped pointing at the roof and gesticulating back and forth as if to be covering the entire mall with his instructions.

Without saying a word, the shadow grabbed the toolbox, and slowly climbed up the ladder and walked over to his partner. He did exactly as Pete Stuart directed. Tim Johnson had heard every word. He pulled out his Glock and checked the chamber carefully, holding the gun in front of him just under the front of the driver's seat. He took a deep breath and looked out at the shoppers. Everything should happen so no one got hurt.

"Where the hell are you, Moore?" Johnson whispered.

40

Hal Barnes was resting in the ER at George Washington University Medical Center. The IVs and monitors were making the correct noises for anyone who might pass by. He sat up in bed, rehearsing his speech over and over. He kept wiping away tears as he practiced.

"Mr. Barnes, are you all right?" a nurse asked as she came in to check his status. She stood at the laptop as she asked.

"Yes. Yes, I'm fine. Thank you. Has Senator Henry called?" Barnes adjusted his position. His heavy body kept sliding down with the back of the bed cranked up.

"Here, let me help you." The nurse adjusted the bed and rearranged his pillows. She pulled up his sheet and blanket to where they lay perfectly across his chest.

"Thank you, but please, has he called?" Barnes was almost pleading.

"I don't know. Let me check." The nurse walked out of the room.

41

Parker's car was slowed by traffic on US-31. "Come on! Jesus!" He was exasperated; the adrenalin had kicked in. Petoskey would be the spot.

"Hang in there, Parker. You should have probably gone the long way around the Bay View Country Club and up Division. Less traffic." Ramsey was a few cars behind him.

"Shut the fuck up. Like you live here." Parker barked into the void of his car. "Sorry, Todd. Nerves, I guess. Just another day at the office for you." Parker looked over at the bay. The clouds were getting darker and rain was just off the horizon and heading inland. He could see the sweeps of gray as they muddled the view toward Bay Harbor.

"It's okay, Parker. I apologize now for the federal government using you as bait. Wouldn't be my call."

"Thanks, Todd. Not the first time they chewed on my ass. Maybe this time I'll get points on my side." Parker passed the light by the Lockwood Building. It was to be razed after the beginning of the year. He hoped he was going to be around to watch.

The white Audi never moved. The occupant finally got out and made her way toward Kmart. She never glanced at the lower lot; she looked like any other shopper going about her business.

Stuart and his team tracked her all the way to the door. He slowly walked away from the van and looked on the roof for his partners. He noticed one standing by the heating unit, looking toward the upper parking lot. He didn't see the other one. As he glanced back toward the Kmart entrance, Stuart saw the woman coming out of the store. Her pace was quicker. He turned quickly to evade eye contact and walked back toward the van. He pulled out a piece of paper from his coat pocket and feigned looking at it as if it was important.

Just before he reached the van he noticed Parker's Fusion coming around the top of the lower lot along the grassy knoll separating the upper lot. Before he could react, the woman started to race down the slope in her dress and heels toward Parker's car.

"Shit, something's coming down." Stuart threw the paper to the ground and reached for his weapon under his coat.

Johnson threw open the car door and hit the side of the white truck parked next to him. The black paint made a large mark on the white door.

"Hey, what the fuck?" said the owner of the truck, who was returning with a package in his arms. He watched Johnson run out between the cars. "Where the hell are you going?" The man dropped his package and chased Johnson. He didn't see the gun in Johnson's hand.

The Suburban was stuck at the light on Sheridan and US-131. Suddenly Ramsey drove around the two cars in front of him. He almost hit one oncoming car, and just missed another as he turned onto Sheridan, came down the hill, and into the lot between Glen's and Garfield's.

"Watch her. Watch her!" Ramsey yelled.

All she carried was a small clutch. She banged on Parker's window.

"Catherine?" He stopped the car.

"No, Moore! No!" Ramsey was yelling in his ear.

Before Parker could react to Ramsey's warning, the passenger door was opened and Catherine was inside. Parker stopped. She kissed him on the cheek. "Just wanted to say good-bye, Parker, before I left." She smiled, jumped out of the car, and dropped her clutch between the door and the passenger seat.

Pete Stuart was almost to Parker and Johnson was rounding a row of cars still being chased by the driver of the white truck.

"Out of the car, Moore! NOW! Out!!" Ramsey was in everyone's ears.

Parker quickly opened his door and flung himself onto the pavement. Pete Stuart knelt down on one knee with his weapon up. Parker rolled right into him. Johnson came up behind and felt a tug on his shoulder from the man chasing him.

Catherine, now minus heels, had run up the slope of the knoll and was jumping into the side of a silver minivan. A man on the roof took a shot that pierced the side of the van. With the door closing, the van quickly turned right, and headed out the west entrance of the lot.

"Rocco, what the hell are you doing?" Laura was in the front passenger seat watching in amazement.

"Sorry, pretty lady." He reached down and brought up his .45.

Before he could pull the trigger, Laura opened her door and jumped out. She landed on a parked car and rolled on its hood, coming to rest with her abdomen against the windshield.

Catherine pulled herself up front and sat in the passenger seat. She cocked a .45 Colt and held it in her lap, then pushed a button on her cell phone. She hadn't seen Parker jump out of the car.

At that instant, the silver Fusion exploded. Stuart fell over Parker and Johnson and the owner of the truck were blown backwards.

42

"Hold your fire! Hold your fire!" Ramsey was yelling into everyone's ear as he raced the Suburban up the short knoll and onto the pavement of the upper lot. He blocked the minivan just before it made another right turn up the long driveway to US-131.

Parker lifted his head and turned around to see the two vehicles collide. It wasn't like the movies. No explosions. No loud, fast music right before impact. Just the crushing sound of metal and glass shattering—then silence. Some steam came from the minivan's engine.

Rocco kicked his door open and came out with his weapon in his right hand. Todd Ramsey was lifting his head up, trying to knock down the airbag. Just as he was able to move the bag, he saw Rocco's head explode. The rooftop shadow didn't miss.

Catherine was trying to get one of the back doors open. Before she figured it out, Todd Ramsey was out and holding his Glock at the side door. "Hello, ma'am. You look familiar."

Catherine was bloody and shaken. Instead of putting up a fight, she sat on the floor between the middle seats.

Parker and Pete Stuart ran toward Ramsey. The man, who had been chasing Johnson, was sitting next to the Public Safety Director on a grassy island in the parking lot.

"Is there something I can help you with?" Johnson asked. His gun was still in his left hand as he leaned back on his elbows.

Without saying a word, the man stood up and ran back to his car. He never looked back. People were coming out of shops and stores. Johnson heard sirens and looked around. The two men on the roof were coming down the ladder. Tim Johnson stood up and brushed off his trench coat. When he looked up, he saw Parker Moore, Pete Stuart, and Todd Ramsey walking toward him with a woman in handcuffs.

"Moore, I'm telling you. Move to Russia. Please?" Johnson was still brushing debris from his trench coat.

"I'm tellin' ya, they won't have me." Parker's face was blank. "Is that it, Agent Ramsey?" He looked over at the NSA agent.

"Yes, Parker. This should do it. Director, I've got to get Parker to the airport. Do you need us around here anymore?" Ramsey was holding Catherine by her arms behind her back.

"Do we take her?" Johnson asked.

"Please. We'll have some U.S. Marshals here for transport in the morning." Ramsey turned to the Michigan State Police officers who were gathered around. "Thanks, Pete. Thanks, you guys."

"No problem. A little more exciting than guarding the governor." Pete Stuart shook Ramsey's hand.

Johnson had moved from the group and was coordinating all the police, rescue, and fire personnel.

"Call the M.E. We'll need him, too," he said to one of the public safety officers walking toward the group. He turned to Parker and shook his hand as he passed by. "See you later, Parker. Take the wife's car. I'll come get it at the airport."

Just before the men departed, Laura came from behind Parker and slugged Ramsey in the jaw. "I hope you all burn in hell." She walked away. One heel was broken and her torn skirt showed her legs right up to her butt. There was no underwear.

It was 5:03 p.m.

43

The nurse poked her head into the room. "Mr. Barnes, Senator Henry is here to see you. Thought that might make you feel better."

"Thank you." Hal Barnes had slid down the bed again. His IVs and monitors were still running, but his potassium and blood sugar levels had not stabilized.

"Hal, my old friend. How are you feeling?" Senator Henry entered the room and removed his topcoat.

"David, please, sit." Barnes was still trying to scoot up, but couldn't. The senator helped Barnes with his pillows. Barnes grabbed the senator's hands. He held them tight and brought David Henry closer. "David, I need to tell you something, but I'm afraid I might be killed for it."

"Hal. It's okay." Senator Henry's delay in arriving at the hospital was because of a call he received from John Mansfield. Both witnesses were secure and the person connected to the security company was in custody.

"I don't know how to say this; so I'll just pretend we are back home in Georgia at our favorite diner." Barnes was stammering, even after rehearsing what he would say over and over again. "I've been bought. Took money under the table— but they threatened you. They threatened me. Those affairs we had years ago—the girl who got pregnant. It was all going to come out. I did it for us. Once they offered money to ease the pain, well, I took it— you'll find it in this account." Barnes gave a slip of paper with a bank name and numbers written on it to the senator. "I didn't spend a dime."

"Hal … I don't know what to say."

"They killed Fairchild. They killed Stimson."

"Hal, I can take care of this. Are you willing to testify?" Senator Henry was a well-respected prosecutor in Georgia and as Chair of the Senate Select Committee on Intelligence he felt confident about making a deal for his oldest friend.

"Yes." Barnes was stoic now. The emotion gone. He was leaning to his left, looking at the senator sitting in a side chair next to the bed.

"Good. Don't worry. You'll be fine. Now, what else?" Senator Henry sat back and listened.

The Learjet 45XR taxied away from the hangar at Pellston Airport, where Todd Ramsey had taken Parker. After a call to his director, Ramsey's last assignment was to get Parker Moore to Fort Meade as fast as possible and to avoid contact with anyone.

"Tell me Todd, why didn't Fairchild—Simon—whatever his name was, kill me the first time he met me? Why the delay?" Parker slouched in a comfortable executive seat on the plane across a small table from Ramsey.

"We assume they didn't know you were the only one in that room at the Silverbow Inn and they wanted to make sure. Their previous contact ratted you out from the intel he got from Henry. I tracked Simon all the way from Corsica to Arizona. It was just luck that we were already suspicious of the oil guys buying a major security company protecting their international interests. These are bad folks, Moore."

Parker looked out the window. The sunset could be seen over the horizon as the plane climbed. He had checked his phone on the way to the airport, after he called Sam's friend Kathi to watch the cats. There were three text messages:

Hi honey. Hope you're having a good day.

Miss you.

Off to the stores with Harrison. Call tonight.

There was only one voicemail from the clinic at the Crest View Mall wondering what had happened. Parker didn't want to talk with anyone but Sam. He knew he'd have to wait. His last request for Johnson was a bottle of Ardbeg 10 year single malt from Gurney's. It was the last of the Islay scotches he had yet to taste.

"What day is this?"

Ramsey did not respond.

Parker looked over at Ramsey. The man was sleeping soundly. "I think it's still Thursday. Wow. This has to be the longest day of the year." Parker just talked to Ramsey as if he was awake. Parker rubbed his chin. It felt itchy. He realized he had a seven-day shadow.

By the time the Learjet had reached cruising altitude, both men were asleep.

44

"Gentlemen, we'll have a short taxi before you can get off. It's 7:46 p.m. Eastern Standard Time. You'll be met by escorts from Fort Meade; they will transport you to Annapolis." The captain made the short announcement soon after he landed the jet. The 45XR made the trip quicker than any commercial airlines and had no clearances to worry about.

"Ready?" Ramsey looked over at Parker.

"Yup." Parker stretched arms, legs, and anything he could.

The aircraft rolled to a stop, the door opened, and the steps were quickly extended. Parker and Ramsey shook the crews' hands as they exited. Parker immediately noticed three GMC Suburbans parked nearby on the tarmac.

"Mr. Moore, I'm John Mansfield. It's a pleasure to meet you." They shook hands.

Parker was surprised by Mansfield's appearance. The Director was disheveled and wearing the same clothes as when he met with Jack Fletcher earlier in the day. A slight breeze blew his wispy hair around like a hairdryer.

"These are the U.S. Marshals who will be with you the next couple of days." He pointed to the suited gentlemen behind him. "I know you have lots of questions and, I promise you, I have lots of answers; but please, let's talk in the morning. I need some sleep, and I'm sure you do as well."

Mansfield ushered Ramsey and Parker toward the middle Suburban. Once everyone was in, the three SUVs drove toward Annapolis Road.

Parker texted Sam:

Exhausted. Going to bed early. Love you.

Parker turned around to look at Ramsey. "Is it still Thursday?"

"Yes," Ramsey said, staring straight ahead.

It was 5:15 a.m. (already Friday) in Dubai. The air was cool and the fog had rolled in. Sir Edward Framingham and Jim Reegan were hooded, had duct tape over their mouths, and their wrists were tied with plastic wire. They sat on the floor of the first-level basement of 23 Marina. The builders of the tallest residential structure in the world, the Hiranandani Group of Mumbai, India, had been very forthcoming with the schematics. This area was directly near a ramp exit; perfect for the van.

The two suited Delta Force men stood near their captives, whispering in Arabic. The garage door opened, and the third Delta Force member in jeans motioned that the van was ready. The darkness and the thick fog provided a perfect cover.

Tim Johnson plopped down on the sofa. He had brought home a large pizza from the Little Caesar's joint at the Crest View Mall. His wife was getting two beers from the fridge. She sat one down in front of him on the coffee table while she kissed him on the head. The house phone rang. Johnson reached over and picked it up from the side table. He turned the TV down at the same time with the remote in his other hand.

"Johnson." He quickly swallowed his first bite of pizza.

"Are you gonna give me the goddamned details now, or what?" Harvey Snow yelled. "This whole week has been a disaster for us because of you. We're behind in covering everything."

"Harvey, I've been a bit busy. I don't even know what day it—"

"It's goddamn Thursday!" Snow cut him off.

"Okay. Be at my office tomorrow at eight and I'll give you the story."

Tim Johnson didn't wait for a reply. He hung up, grabbed his beer and the remote, and turned up the TV while taking a long swig of his favorite Bell's Two Hearted IPA. His wife sat beside him and drank her beer right along with him.

45

FRIDAY ~ OCTOBER 28

The drive to the NSA building at Fort Meade was a short one. Done under the cover of early morning darkness, the Suburban pulled up to the curb and Parker stepped out with his three new shadows. His sleep had been restless and he had not bothered to shower or change out of his clothes, for that matter. So many conversations passed through his mind that he woke up with a headache. Parker knew it was pure emotion since the pain was centered behind his forehead.

This was about Senator Stimson's death. It was about something that Parker never would have thought was important, but someone else did. He couldn't stop thinking about the conversation he overheard at the Silverbow Inn in Juneau between the Brit and the Texan; the Alaska governor's new security staff; and Stimson's secretary with the clipboard. For some reason the Super PAC Parker had worked for was active again.

At that same time, Parker was struggling to free himself of his abusive second wife. Journaling helped. He suspected no one knew he wrote down everything he heard and witnessed except for the missing six months. Parker had one of the old journals with him now. Ramsey had allowed Parker to quickly stop by the house before they headed to Pellston Airport so Parker could grab some clothes. Parker also ran down to his studio and grabbed the tattered Moleskin.

Parker walked into the front lobby of NSA headquarters and looked around, acting as most first-time visitors do. The three plain clothed marshals stood nearby.

"Parker. It's again a pleasure. Follow me." John Mansfield led Parker through security and up to his offices. He dismissed the marshals. "Thanks, gentlemen. I'll call you when we're finished. I suspect it will be close to lunchtime." One of the Marshals handed Mansfield a business card.

Not much had changed in Mansfield's appearance. Messed hair and same old cardigan and Dockers, but he was wearing a clean polo shirt to indicate he had gone home before returning to the office at 5:00 a.m.

After exiting the elevator on the fourth floor, they met Kirk, Mansfield's personal assistant. He was putting papers into Eye's Only folders and noticed Parker's ripped shirt and dirty pants. "Chief, you want I get Mr. Moore some clothes for today?" Kirk smiled and shook his head as he looked Parker up and down.

"Actually, no, if Parker doesn't mind I'd like to exhibit what he's been through physically and emotionally—although dressing up would help appearances, I suppose. This is supposed to be an unannounced emergency meeting; so let's not go overboard." Mansfield turned toward Parker and expected a reply.

"No problem, sir. I'm afraid to say that this would be close to my regular weekend attire anyway, but I did grab some clean clothes before we left Petoskey." Parker didn't know whether to smile or be embarrassed. He looked himself over and shrugged. "How about some breakfast? That I'll take."

"Good idea. We're gonna be a while," Mansfield said as he looked at Kirk.

"At 5:30 in the morning, I'm not sure what I can find; but I'll do my best," Kirk said. He left the room, closing the door behind him.

Several floors below John Mansfield's office, the Super PAC was being briefed by his boss, NSA Director Grant Holloway. Five of the six people were adroitly dressed as always, even at this early hour. Senator Henry was another matter.

"So," said the leader as she put down her coffee and grabbed a slip of paper in front of her. "For Christ's sake, David, you look terrible." She took a moment to look at the good senator, then back to the paper she held. "We have Mr. Moore. Seems like he has nine lives." She shook her head with a sigh as she looked at everyone around the small round table. "We have Mr. Brooks. We have U.S. Marshals bringing in the surviving assassin who was out to kill Mr. Moore. What about our men from Dubai?" She looked at Holloway.

"One's on his way. The other—well, let's just say that if we have problems with the extradition, he still might be out of action," Holloway answered with a grin.

"This is funny?" she asked with a stoic look.

"Actually, yes," he said firmly as he smiled and looked around the table at everyone. It was difficult for him to hold back his laughter. The Attorney General and Senator Henry had to cover their mouths in a poor attempt at discreetness as they looked at each other.

The leader just smiled.

Still in Dubai, Sir Edward was awakening from a deep sleep he'd been in for several hours. As he looked around, he had no idea where he was, and he had no idea who the two women were who were with him on the bed, moving around at the direction of a photographer. One was naked and the other wore very seductive black lingerie. The room had some filtered light, and he was on a very large bed

"Hello, there, Sir Edward. We're so glad you're here." said the naked woman now lying next to him. She spoke English with a seductive French accent.

Sir Edward felt so drowsy he wasn't able to respond or even move his body. The photographer left and the women got up and went into an adjoining room. Sir Edward fell back asleep.

Jim Reegan had never been afraid of anything—until now. He was looking across a bench at two men in FBI windbreakers. One was Jack Fletcher, who had arrested Reegan on suspicion of murder and conspiracy to commit murder, along with a host of other charges he was still trying to comprehend. The only thing he remembered about being kidnapped from 23 Marina was being grabbed and hooded by men speaking Arabic. Now he was on a small jet taxiing onto the runway at Ramstein Air Force Base in Germany on his way to Washington D.C. Suddenly, a trillion dollars seemed trivial.

Senator David Henry was finishing his part of the briefing for the Intelligence Committee hearing to be held later in the day. "Hal Barnes broke down and explained the bribery of Mark Fairchild. They took a different tactic with Hal by starting with threats, but eventually they slowly began bribing him with money. By the way, Fairchild's killer may be the same woman from the Petoskey arrest."

"Okay," began the woman leading the Super PAC, "I believe the policy of our group to use minimal or diversionary information has allowed our integrity to remain intact. Please continue to vet your staffs to the highest degree. And, thank you Mr. Holloway for your staff's assistance in that. Has the Vice President been informed of the hearing?"

"Yes. He knows we're going to call it today and not Saturday or Sunday as our communications had indicated." Senator Henry looked tired. He'd been with Hal Barnes at the hospital until midnight, and decided to spend the night in his office instead of going home. Henry hadn't seen Parker Moore or John Mansfield yet—his attire would fit in well with the other torn and tattered pieces to the puzzle.

"Anything else, gentlemen?" asked their leader as she surveyed the others. Everyone looked at each other but no one said anything.

In the next moment, all heads shook no. "Fine. See you at three p.m. at Hart. You all know your places. Nice work, everyone." She got up and left the room. The others chatted as they stood up and began to exit.

"Senator," Grant Holloway lightly grabbed David Henry by the right elbow. "I'm sorry about your friend Mr. Barnes. I must admit, we didn't see that one coming."

"That's okay, Director. I didn't either. I'm going to try and take a nap." The two shook hands and Holloway patted the senator on his back as they closed the door behind them.

46

John Mansfield's office was still cluttered with maps, papers, books, and the ever present laptop in the middle of the table next to the desk. In the background, Leonard Bernstein played Gershwin's *Rhapsody in Blue*. Parker Moore sat where Jack Fletcher was the day before. He was eating a whole wheat bagel with plain cream cheese while Mansfield scooped the last of his yogurt out of the container. The sunlight was just beginning to rise above the trees surrounding the Fort Meade building as another Suburban pulled in front and dropped off four men.

"So, what I'm trying to comprehend is that Stimson was killed because he was working both sides of the fence?" Parker asked Mansfield in between bites of his bagel.

"Yes. Stimson worked with the Super PAC until he felt his colleagues ushered him out in disgrace; then he turned to the other side. The oil and gas lobby was with him for years, and this was exactly what they were waiting for. As a matter of fact, we now know the Dubai-centered super PAC was using money to push Stimson's departure from the Senate. We have implicated twenty-four House members, ten senators, one Supreme Court Justice—and more worrisome than that—two Republican presidential candidates who have entered the primaries. The Dubai group has influence in two branches and wants the third. When we go public with our findings, things are going to get pretty chaotic. Your discussion with Stimson was one of the items the Super PAC needed; however once Stimson went over to the bad guys, he told them all about you and that you were in the Silverbow listening."

It was as if the world had been lifted off Parker's shoulders.

He felt his entire body lighten. The sun coming in through the window and shining on the maps and papers was like a searchlight that located a hidden treasure. For one week, Parker had been thrown into a catastrophic storm. For one week, he was back into a numbing process of departure from reality. And, with one small revelation of something that happened four years ago, he knew he wasn't crazy—and he wasn't going to lose everything again. Parker Moore knew everything was going to be all right.

"The Silverbow," Parker said. "The Silverbow. Juneau," he repeated. "They're the bad guys, aren't they? Those two sons-of-bitches are the ones who tried to kill me?" He felt emotion. Anger that seemed healthy and not out of place within his recovery.

"Yes. Sir Edward Framingham and Jim Reegan. They built an empire of oil, banking, and a few government agencies in select countries, then connected them into a super political action committee. The funds were housed in a Swiss bank account, which included some money going into those countries and companies from the United States—monies approved by the House and Senate. They paid the money through dummy corporations set up in the Cayman Islands. The pain you experienced, Parker, and the troubles you encountered were not in vain. You have helped put a horrible system before the public eye." John Mansfield was leaning over his desk and seemed to lean further forward the more Parker leaned backward in a slumping reaction to what he was hearing. "Parker, we can't fix what has happened to you, but we can all move on now."

Mansfield got up and walked over to an antique oak corner cabinet. He opened the double doors. The interior held a bar fit for a connoisseur of any fine liquor—and some not-so-fine. He grabbed a bottle of Ardbeg single malt and held the dark green labeled bottle up to Parker. Parker nodded with a grin as he got up and walked over to the window. In any stressful situation, Parker always turned to the outdoors, but the view out of the fourth-floor window was the best he could do at this moment.

"I've always wanted to make an impact. I always wanted to make a difference," Parker said.

Mansfield tore off the top paper from the bottle and twisted off the cork. The simple sound of the popping cork made Parker turn and walk over to the cabinet. Mansfield poured two fingers in two crystal scotch glasses and handed one to Parker.

"Islay's are my favorite as well," Mansfield said as he held up his glass while looking through it with one eye closed as the sun's rays pierced the fine malted whiskey. He swirled the glass ever so gently then clinked his glass with Parker's.

The week of killings and attempted killings, the week of not knowing what was real or who to trust, the car explosion—it all came rushing forward. As Parker sipped, the seaweed and peat wafted into his olfactory memory and created a soothing memory of sitting in his Petoskey writing studio. It felt like weeks since he had sat and connected with his own thoughts. He noticed his hand shaking. At that moment, his phone vibrated in his pocket. He caught himself in mid-thought and opened his phone:

Morning honey.

He set the glass on top of some papers on the table and texted back as he smiled:

Morning doll.

He returned to gaze out the window as his hand steadied. Sam could calm him from anywhere on the globe.

"Parker? You okay? Everything okay on the phone?" Mansfield was back in his tattered chair with the duct-taped arms. His head was cocked to the left as he smiled.

"Yes. I'm okay. It was Sam." Parker turned from the window and sat back down in the chair. "What do you need me to do?"

47

It was 9:00 a.m. John Brooks sat in a NSA conference room with his feet up on the table; Todd Ramsey sat across from him in a chair while using another as a footstool. The two were catching up. At one point, Ramsey was laughing so hard, he had to take his feet off the chair as he bent over to catch his breath.

"Stop. Stop!" Ramsey said. "A brothel in Dubai? That's priceless!"

"We couldn't get extradition set quickly enough; so we figured the guys could give him an afternoon etched in the threat of YouTube." John Brooks could barely get the words out before he started laughing again.

"I got to hand it to you; that's something right out of a Bond movie. In fact—" Ramsey was stopped short when the door opened and in walked John Mansfield.

"Boys, let me introduce you to ..." The director smiled as Parker walked in behind him.

Brooks yanked his feet off the table and jumped out of his chair. He ran around the table and shook Parker's hand and hugged him at the same time. Both men smiled. Ramsey stayed in his chair. He smiled as he looked at Mansfield who had moved aside.

"Moore, you son of a bitch! How many lives you got anyway?" John Brooks stood in front of Parker with his hands on Parker's shoulders like a father would do to a son—even though Parker had ten years and five inches on Brooks.

"Left? I got three or four left, but as long as you guys are around, maybe more." Parker smiled softly. His affection for these two men far outweighed the anger and animosity he felt four years ago. "Did you know I flipped you off as you walked away from me that day on the Mall in D.C., Mr. Brooks?"

"Of course I did. We had someone taking pictures of the whole meeting. I deserved it. Good to see you, Parker. Good to see you."

The four men sat down as Kirk brought in coffee and donuts.

"The Dunkin' Donuts opened. Thought it would be a nice treat," Kirk said as he set down a box of two dozen assorted donuts and four black coffees. Ramsey and Parker grabbed for the box as if they hadn't eaten in a week. Kirk began to leave the room.

"It's been one long, fucking week," said Ramsey as he stuffed a sour cream donut in his mouth.

"Kirk. Stay. Let's get this finished, so we can all go home and get cleaned up. Senator Henry will be here soon." John Mansfield carefully removed the plastic white lid from a coffee and blew at the steaming black liquid as if it were just any other day in the office.

48

The Marble Room on the Senate side of the Capitol in Washington D.C. adjoined the Senate lobby. It was 1:15 p.m. The fifteen members of the Senate Select Committee on Intelligence were gathered for a rare public meeting, but first they were being briefed by the Chair of the Committee, Senator David Henry. The light lunch and reception offered an informal meeting prior to what could be the most remembered day since 9/11.

The eight Democrats and seven Republicans mingled without design to partisanship. They were aware of what lay before them. Staffers of the committee members moved in and out of the small groups to grab plates of sandwiches and other finger foods from the servers as they strolled by. Senator Henry, standing in the middle of the room, gestured for everyone to gather near.

"Colleagues and friends, what will happen today is unprecedented in our history. What may come from this hearing and the investigations that will continue, will shape the very essence of our democracy. I chose this reception area for a reason." He continued to speak as he slowly turned three hundred and sixty degrees to make eye-to-eye contact with everyone. "Within this building, where President Wilson said *'The world must be made safe for democracy'* and President Roosevelt talked of a *'date which will live in infamy'*, America was protected and crafted ever so elegantly to allow every man, woman, and child a voice. A voice to mold their country as they so choose.

"We've lost that voice. Our mission and our focus in this public forum is to hear testimony on intelligence matters involving the clear and present danger to us from abroad; and, unfortunately, from within our own borders. I ask that you not waiver from this duty. Our elected government must not and will not become the puppet of a destructive force demeaning the citizens who place their trust in you. As you hear the testimony today, and we make decisions to proceed, you are well aware that some of your colleagues will not leave this building unscathed. They will face the wrath and the justice provided by our Constitution and the civil liberties upon which they took their oath.

"At 3:00 p.m. we will be a part of history—I thank you for that honor and—," Senator Henry found himself emotionally charged and choked with tears. "—the privilege to right the wrongs we have *all* participated in."

There was silence.

Senator Henry and some of his staff, slowly made their way toward the doors that led into the formal office of the Vice President. The remaining people watched in silence. One by one they put down whatever dish or glass they held and made their way to the long tunnel that led to the Hart Senate Office Building.

"I haven't eaten here in so long. It's still loud, tight, and perfect." Parker was stuffing pancakes, eggs, and bacon in his mouth as fast as he could.

He sat with John Brooks and Todd Ramsey in a tight booth at Pete's Diner in the Capitol Hill/Southeast neighborhood of Washington D.C. They were all wearing suits, but Parker and Ramsey still looked tired. Six U.S. Marshals were sitting at the counter having their own lunch, while the Secret Service stood outside the restaurant and made sure no one entered. Senator Henry had made arrangements for the men after he met with them that morning.

"It's about time we made our way over to Hart." Todd Ramsey was sitting back looking up at the clock behind the counter. It was 1:30 p.m.

"Yeah, Parker, you done?" John Brooks asked. "I can't believe the way you eat. It's a constant."

"Yes," said Parker as he took his last drink of orange juice. His six-foot, five-inch frame barely fit in the booth. "What day is this?" he asked as he stood and made his way to the door behind the U.S. Marshals.

"Friday. Why?" Brooks asked.

"How did you put it ,Todd? It's been one long, fucking week." Parker stepped into the Suburban behind Ramsey and Brooks.

The three Suburbans headed to the Hart Senate Office Building across the street from the United States Supreme Court, where Jack Fletcher was walking up the steps with three other suited FBI Agents and the FBI Director. None were talking or smiling. The Justices were meeting in a closed session today.

49

"I call this meeting to order . . ." Senator Henry sat on the middle bench while the other members sat behind and around him in the hearing room. Staffers and pages were seated toward the back behind the press section. Some made phone calls, shuffled papers, and gazed into laptops, tablets, and phones. It was straight up 3:00 p.m. Eastern Standard Time.

The press was settling in after rushing to make the hearing. The notice had only been posted an hour ago. Camera crew and reporters were still setting up as Senator Henry began. At the witness table in front of the center bench, sat John Brooks, Parker Moore, and two attorneys from the Justice Department. In the very back of the room sat the U.S. Attorney General and several rows away was the Director of NSA, Grant Holloway. Over in the far corner, standing against the wall, was the leader of the Super PAC. No one seemed surprised she was there, but no one stood around her either, except three Secret Service Agents. To the left of the witness table three people were seated. A throng of suited FBI and U.S. Marshals surrounded them. Jim Reegan, Jack Fletcher, and Catherine Hamilton sat quietly and stared at the witnesses.

"Mr. Parker Moore and Mr. John Brooks, do you solemnly swear to tell the truth before this committee, so help you God?"

"I do." Both men spoke simultaneously.

"Consider yourselves under oath," Senator David Henry replied.

50

SATURDAY ~ OCTOBER 29

Parker was face down on the bed between two pillows. His soft snore was ignored by Kali as she licked the finger of his left hand as it protruded out from the covers near the nightstand on Sam's side of the bed. Keeper watched from the doorway. A half-empty bottle of Ardbeg scotch was on the dining room table with a crystal glass sitting next to it. Mozart's *Piano Concerto Number 23* played repeatedly on the stereo.

All at once, both cats dashed into the upstairs hall and down the stairs.

"Parker? Parker?" Sam walked into the kitchen carrying her black carry-on luggage. "Hey, you guys! Did you miss me?" She stopped and picked up Kali and brought the feline eye level.

Parker did not move. His snoring continued. As Sam walked through the kitchen and into the dining room, she spotted the scotch and the glass. She smiled and shook her head. The cats were rubbing against her legs since they hadn't been fed or let outside yet for the morning. It was 10:07 a.m. on the microwave clock. Sam turned left into the reading room and turned off the stereo.

"Parker!" she yelled as she started walking upstairs. Once reaching the bedroom doorway, she dropped her bag and jumped on the bed. "Parker Moore, kiss me!"

"Ow! Is that any way to wake me up?" Parker still hadn't moved. Sam sat on top of him. "Okay. Okay." He turned over, careful not to bump her off the bed. Sam bent over and kissed him. "It's good to have you home, Sam."

“Parker, did you shave at all since I left? That’s about a nine-day shadow.”

Parker felt his face and realized he hadn’t shaved, not even for the hearing.

“No. I guess I didn’t.” He sat up and leaned against the headboard. Sam was at her closet and opening the door. She set the carry-on inside and closed the door.

“Well, get your butt up. It’s Saturday and we need to have some fun. By the looks of you and that scotch bottle downstairs I bet you’ve been lazy all week.” She was talking as she made her way down the stairs. The floor boards squeaked. “I see you fixed the floor,” she said sarcastically. “Lazy ass.” She was smiling.

Parker moved to the side of the bed and sat up. His hands rested on the bed at his side. The unseasonably warm breeze that came through the slightly opened window that Tim Johnson had repaired felt good. He looked to where only a few days ago, a man lay after trying to kill him.

He heard Sam say it was Saturday—but he was still trying to get everything straight in his mind. He rubbed his chin and headed toward the bathroom for a shower.

“Parker,” Sam yelled from downstairs, “where’s your car?”

Don't miss Book 3 of the Parker Moore Series.

Turn the page for a preview ...

Two years have passed since Parker Moore was last involved in a high-stakes game with the Super PAC from Dubai ...

"Gray is dead," Parker whispered to himself.

He turned quietly to walk along the tree line by the fracking well and inched through pine boughs. Noticing cameras around the perimeter, he was careful to avoid them. Getting closer wouldn't change what he saw from his vantage point. He'd seen enough, and it was time to retrieve Sam.

Turning around to his left with his head down to avoid a fallen tree, Parker suddenly felt a thud against his left temple. His left ear was somewhere between ringing and deaf. The thicket of dead branches below the canopy stuck out from the tree trunks, and he felt one tear into his side as he fell. Eyes closed, he tried to open them and collect himself. Instantly he thought it was a bear.

With his right ear, he heard twigs breaking, and then he realized he wasn't moving. From his knees, he rose quickly as he opened his eyes and saw the hulk of a man romping toward him.

Parker lowered himself like a linebacker breaking down to tackle a fullback head-on. He caught the man in his midsection and drove him back through a thicket of jack pine. Branches were cracking as loud as the man groaned. Parker's shoulder ramming the attacker's lower sternum and diaphragm had knocked the wind out of him as he hurdled backwards.

Keeping his fists clenched, Parker had wrapped his arms around the massive midsection of the assailant and could feel the dead pine branches cutting into his knuckles. He drove the man downward into the mud and slush. There was a loud thud; Parker could feel the vibration of the ground and the air leaving the man's lungs. He was afraid he'd killed him. Parker looked at the older man before him. His eyes were closed and his face grimaced—but Parker could feel air return to the man's chest.

The bright moon showed only a glint of some snow pack under the trees in front of them, but it was enough to expose some tree trunks and a path. Parker pushed hard on the chest of the attacker to make sure he lost air again, and launched himself forward through the woody undergrowth and disappeared into the forest. His adrenalin didn't allow for pain, and he made a quick glance back to see no one was following.

Knowing the area well, Parker ran east. He needed to get to the river to make better sense of where he was exactly. He paused to listen. Only the low hum of the generator and pumps. The forest was dark behind him.

Keeping a quick and steady pace after the pause, Parker found the river and immediately thought he knew where he was. One foot into the deep muck; then the other. A shorter distance to water, but as he heard and felt the sucking sound of the soft blackness around his right lower leg behind him, the frigid water stung his left leg in front. He'd stepped into a deep hole along the current of an outside back-flow. The water was up to his neck as the rear leg exited the muck. The cold startled him out of the fog he hadn't realized enveloped him after the blow to his head.

He shook his head and took a few deep breaths. He was out of the hole in two steps. The water, now ankle deep, allowed him to take four long strides to the eastern bank. The fishing path along the river going south took him directly to the Trout Unlimited area he originally entered.

Sam! he thought. Then he caught himself. She'll be okay. His hands resting on his knees, dripping wet, he lifted his head to look and listen for anything beyond the soft gurgling stream. Nothing .

Pain. Stabbing and throbbing pain. The adrenalin was wearing off, allowing him to feel the pain below his ribs and along his right side. He brought his left hand up and over to feel—a stick was embedded in his side, far enough to hurt but fortunately it hadn't broken through to any vital areas.

As he hiked back to his truck, Parker could feel the chill in his body. The pain of the wood pierced his side, but paradoxically the relief of being close to his vehicle calmed him. Once at the truck, he reached up under the left front fender and grabbed the key. He unlocked the door and retrieved the Swiss Army knife from his faithful backpack. He shut off the dome light and sat along the side of the truck against the right front tire away from the river. His small flashlight held close to the wound provided enough ambient light for him to pull the wood out clean.

"Shit! Sonovabitch!" Parker quietly yelled.

He knocked the back of his head against the fender and quickly remembered the left side of his head was throbbing. He felt around his left ear; the warmth of the blood was exaggerated against the cold of his fingers. He followed another warm trickle down his left cheek and onto his neck. There was already a crust from earlier blood.

He wasn't dizzy but the fog was returning to his thought process. Not enough to dim the desire of getting away safely and returning to Sam. Parker reached forward and gathered some snow to put on his temple. He instantly felt the cold and the searing pain. The lump on the side of his head was palpable.

After taking several more deep breaths, Parker stood up and quietly got inside the truck.

The cell phone showed no signal. Before starting the engine, he turned off the automatic headlights; once started, he quickly tapped the brakes to release the transmission. He felt his clothes squish water on the seat as he began to shiver. He slowly drove southeast onto Manistee River Road and finally turned on the headlights. He saw nothing but blackness in the rearview mirror.

Anger gnawed at him. He had to trust Sam was okay.

ABOUT THE AUTHOR

After working as a professional, educator, executive and lobbyist in health care for thirty-nine years, Stewert James lives a quiet life of volunteering and consulting in Northern Michigan.

www.stewertjames.com